JAN IN INDIA

Books by OAK:

THE PLANET OF PERIL
THE PRINCE OF PERIL
THE PORT OF PERIL

MAZA OF THE MOON

THE SWORDSMAN OF MARS
THE OUTLAWS OF MARS
THE HUNTERS OF MARS (unpublished)

TAM, SON OF THE TIGER
JAN OF THE JUNGLE
JAN IN INDIA

THE MAN WHO LIMPED & OTHER STORIES

OTIS ADELBERT KLINE

JAN IN INDIA

ILLUSTRATIONS BY
STEVE LEIALOHA

FOREWORD & GLOSSARY BY
DAVID ANTHONY KRAFT

FICTIONEER BOOKS LTD.
Lakemont, Georgia 30552
1974

Published by arrangement with
David Anthony Kraft,
Agent for the Literary Estate of
Otis Adelbert Kline.

Printed for Fictioneer Books, Ltd. by
CSA Printing and Bindery
Lakemont, Georgia 30552

CONTENTS

JAN IN INDIA

Foreword by
David Anthony Kraft

OTIS ADELBERT KLINE

Otis Adelbert Kline, author of weird and fantastic adventure stories, was born in Chicago on July 1, 1891. Interested in astronomy and earth science as a child, his avid imagination fed on the fiction of Jules Verne and H. G. Wells. Also fond of music, he wrote several popular songs while still in high school, and experienced the writer's traditional quota of occupations. In his own words, he "bonded rails behind a steel gang . . . hiked poles on toll line repair . . . worked in various factories and a shoe store . . . learned the printing trade . . . became advertising manager of a newspaper . . . worked for two music publishers and owned and operated a music publishing company" in addition to many other endeavors.

Kline was one of very few writers for the great

Weird Tales who had a novelette in the first issue—March, 1923. He continued to appear in its pages for another two decades, as well as contributing to over fifty other American magazines; earlier, he'd done scripts for the infant motion picture industry. Serialization in 1929 of his first interplanetary adventure novel, THE PLANET OF PERIL, in *Argosy All-Story*, brought him wide popularity, and he followed up with five more over a period of four years. The last two, THE SWORDSMAN OF MARS and THE OUTLAWS OF MARS, rank among the most exciting of his works. All six have been published in both hardcover and paperback.

OAK also wrote several other novels, including TAM, SON OF THE TIGER and JAN OF THE JUNGLE. The latter, serialized in *Argosy* in 1931, was retitled CALL OF THE SAVAGE by Universal, who released it as a 12 part movie serial in 1935. Kline's sequel, JAN IN INDIA—a previously unreprinted fantasy-adventure classic culled from the pages of *Argosy*—details the further exploits of Jan Trevor, who falls victim to the treacherous plottings of the Maharajah of Varuda in the steaming tropics of India.

In later years, Otis Adelbert Kline became a literary agent, selling the output of such renowned authors as John W. Campbell, F. Scott Fitzgerald and Robert E. Howard. He became an expert in foreign markets, and his own material appeared in print in Australia, Czechoslovakia, Denmark, England, Finland, France, Holland, Sweden and other countries. At least one of his stories has been adapted for television.

After his death in 1946, of a heart attack, his agency—Otis Kline Associates—changed hands, and a great deal of valuable material was lost or destroyed, including what is said to have been the completed manuscript of a third Mars novel. In recent years, Otis Adelbert Kline's adventure yarns have continued to experience the popularity that is due stories which can utterly captivate the imagination and transport a reader into worlds of high action.

—David Anthony Kraft

CHAPTER 1

A MURDEROUS PLOT

The sun sank, red and sullen, behind the tossing waters of the Bay of Bengal, and the lights of the yacht *Georgia A.* flashed on as the night descended with tropical suddenness.

Under the gay canopy which shaded the fore-deck an after-dinner bridge game was in progress. The four who played were Harry Trevor, American millionaire sportsman and owner of the yacht, a tall, dark-haired man in his early forties; Georgia Trevor, his stately, Titian-haired wife; and their guests, Don Francesco Suarez and Doña Isabella, from Venezuela.

Leaning over the stern rail side by side, but with eyes sullenly aloof from each other, and no thought for the beauty of the Indian night, were Jan Trevor and Ramona Suarez. Like his father, Jan was tall and broad-shouldered, yet he had the auburn hair and blue eyes of his mother. And instead of the stiff, military carriage of the elder Trevor, his was rather the lithe, supple grace of a jungle animal— a grace of movement that had not been cultivated in any drawing-room, but had, rather, been learned from the ocelot, the jaguar and the puma in their

native haunts. For, despite his immaculate tropical evening clothes and the fashionable cut of his hair, Jan was but six months removed from the vast trackless jungle of South America that had mothered him.

Ramona was small and slender, a striking brunette with a slightly Oriental tilt to her big brown eyes, which showed that though she bore the name of Suarez, she was descended from a race much older than that which inhabits the Iberian Peninsula. Just now tears quivered on her long dark lashes, for she and Jan had quarreled for the first time. The quarrel had been trivial enough. This tall, red-headed fiance of hers had been so attentive to her during the six months they had spent on their leisurely round-the-world cruise, that she had become piqued by his in-attention of this evening and had spoken sharply to him.

She gazed out over the water for some time in silence. Then, her mood softening, she turned and laid a hand on his arm.

"Tell me, Jan. What is wrong? What has come over you? Ever since we came within sight of this strange jungle you have paid no attention to me. You go about as one in a dream. Or you hang over the rail, staring, sniffing the air. What has happened to you?"

Jan passed his hand over his eyes. "Ramona, I—I don't know. I have a strange feeling inside me which I cannot understand—a feeling of sadness. I wish I could explain—"

"You need not," she interrupted, her pride aroused. "You have tired of me, Jan, that is it. I know it—can tell it by your every action. It is well that this happened before we were married—that I found it out in time. I will leave you at the next port. Father, mother, and I can take a steamer from Calcutta. Oh, I'm glad! Glad! Do you hear?"

Her last words were uttered in a choking voice, and ended in a muffled sob. Then she turned and sprinted across the deck toward the companionway.

With a single bound, Jan caught her, held her prisoned in his arms. "Ramona, please—" he begged. "You do not understand. I—I—"

She beat upon his breast with her tiny fists, wrenched herself free. "You are a brute, a beast! I hate you!" she sobbed.

Then she darted off and plunged down the companionway.

Standing bewildered by this sudden change in the

girl he had always considered so gentle, Jan waited until he heard the slam of her cabin door. What could he have done to arouse her so? Why should this strange moodiness which had seized him have so startling an effect upon her? And after all, what was it that had suddenly come over him upon their advent in these waters?

He returned to the rail to ponder the perplexing problem, and while he pondered he gazed at the distant jungle over which the gibbous moon was just rising, and from which there came to him strange scents and sounds—strange, yet somehow vaguely familiar.

First, there was the musty odor of decaying wood and leaves, which in every jungle is the same. There was the mingled perfume of many tropical wild flowers which were strange to him. And there were cat scents and cat sounds which he instantly recognized as such, though they were subtly different from those with which he had been familiar in his jungle. There were the calls of night birds, and somewhere a strange beast was trumpeting. Never before had he heard that sound, yet he instinctively knew that only an immense creature could make it.

Jan had never heard of nostalgia, and since he had never had a permanent home, save a cage in a private menagerie, which he hated, it would be difficult to imagine him homesick. Yet the jungle was his home. The jungle had reared him, fed him, mothered him. And while she had taught him many cruel lessons, they had been more than compensated for by the freedom and happiness she had brought him.

And so this alien jungle, which was like his jungle, yet different, had stirred a fierce longing in his heart, a strange, subjective yearning which he was unable to interpret in objective terms. He was drawn as iron is drawn to a lodestone, but he did not realize it. He only knew that he felt a strange sadness, an inexplicable longing; and that for no reason which he could understand, Ramona was angry with him.

As he leaned morosely over the rail, a plump, brown-skinned man who sat in a steamer chair beside the door of the companionway, observed closely for some time. Then he took a lacquered case from beneath his voluminous garments, selected a cigarette, and lighted it, the flare of the match revealing his turbaned head, his round moon-like face, and the generously padded proportions of his short, rotund person.

Scarcely had the yellow flare died down ere a small, wiry figure slunk out from the shadows and crouched beside the chair of the obese one.

"I am here, *babuji*," he said in Urdu.

The fat man did not turn his head, but whispered from the corner of his mouth in the same language.

"The time has come to do what is to be done. See that you do it well. If you fail you will surely die. If you succeed you will not only acquire merit before your black goddess; you will be a rich man as well."

"I will not fail, *babuji*."

"So? Then wait here, my good Kupta, until I again strike a light."

The babu rose ponderously, and tossed his burning cigarette into the water. Then he circled the deck and mounted the ladder to the wheelhouse, where the second officer, Nelson, stood watch.

"Good evening, sair," he said with a profound bow.

"Evening," Nelson replied with a touch of surliness. He was not a man to encourage familiarity from any native, educated or otherwise.

"A cigarette, *sahib*?" the babu proffered his case.

"No, thanks," curtly.

The Indian took one, placed it between his flabby lips. Deliberately he fished out a match.

"Look, gentleman!" he exclaimed suddenly, pointing a chubby finger over the bow. "What is that floating in water ahead of us?"

Nelson gripped the wheel and strained his eyes forward. "Don't see a thing," he grunted.

The babu struck the match.

"Right there in front of us!" he exclaimed. "Looks like an overturned boat."

In the meantime, the small wiry man had been lurking in the shadows, waiting for the signal of the lighted match. He now sprang out and ran swiftly and silently toward the unsuspecting Jan, who still leaned over the rail. In one hand he carried a heavy slung shot. The direction of the breeze was such that the jungle man could not scent the approach of the enemy. And the roar of the propeller drowned any slight noise which might otherwise have come to his acute hearing.

The slung shot whirled aloft, was brought down with sickening force on the wind-tousled red head.

Jan slumped silently over the rail.

His assailant stooped, caught him by the ankles, and heaved. The limp body turned over once, struck the waves with a great splash, the sound of which was muffled by the propeller, and disappeared from view.

A moment later the assassin had melted into the shadows.

Up in the wheelhouse, Nelson was still straining his eyes toward the moon-silvered water ahead. Presently he turned to the babu.

"You must be seeing things," he growled. "Maybe you've got some hashish in those cigarettes."

"Do not use hashish, gentleman," said Babu Chandra Kumar in a hurt tone. Covertly he glanced toward the stern rail. It was deserted. Then with an injured, "Good night, sair," he flung the cigarette into the water, and descended the ladder, whence he waddled slowly back to his steamer chair. As he squeezed his great bulk into that protesting piece of furniture, a voice came from the shadows.

"It is done, *babuji.*"

"Very good, Kupta. I am sure that Kali will bless you. And here are your hundred rupees."

The coins clinked softly in the darkness, and the dusky Kupta once more merged with the shadows.

CHAPTER II

MAN OVERBOARD!

Babu Chandra Kumar remained in his steamer chair for a full half hour. Then he took a small teakwood box from an inside pocket. Opening it, he extracted a bit of betel nut which he rolled in a pan leaf with a pellet of lime and a cardamon seed and thrust into his flabby mouth. Closing the box with a snap, he replaced it in his pocket, rose ponderously, and waddled to the starboard rail, where he stood, expectorating red juice over the side and watching the distant shore line which was plainly visible in the rays of the rising moon.

Presently he saw that for which he had been waiting—a sampan with its sail bellying in the wind about halfway between the yacht and the shore. Swiftly he glanced up at the man in the wheelhouse.

Seeing that his back was turned, he shouted at the top of his voice, "Gentleman! Gentleman! Assistance! Help! Young *sahib* has jumped into the water!"

Nelson swung around.

"What's that?" he bellowed incredulously.

"Young *sahib* ! He leaped into bay! I saw him! He will drown!" shrilled the babu.

''Man overboard!'' the officer sang out.

Then he issued some swift orders.

There was instant confusion on the yacht. Cries of alarm from those on the foredeck mingled with the ringing of bells, the roar of the suddenly reversed screw, and the barking of orders.

The portly, red-faced Captain McGrew, who had been smoking and reading in his cabin, wheezed up the ladder, hastily buttoning his jacket. Harry Trevor and Don Francesco dashed up the opposite ladder.

''Who was it?'' Trevor demanded.

''It was your son, sir, according to the babu. Just now he shouted that the young *sahib* had leaped overboard.''

''Good God! Jan? It seems incredible!''

''Bring her about! Break out lines and life preservers and man the rails! Stand by to lower a lifeboat,'' barked Captain McGrew.

Trevor and Don Francesco hurried to the foredeck once more to join the ladies. As they did so, Ramona came running up, her eyes red with weeping.

''What happened?'' she asked. ''I heard shouts, and the engines stopped.''

''The babu says he just saw Jan jump overboard,'' said Trevor.

At this announcement Georgia Trevor went deathly white. Her husband passed a supporting arm around her.

''There, there. Don't be alarmed,'' he said, trying to hide his own concern. ''The boy is a strong swimmer. Probably just leaped overboard for a lark. There's no danger. We'll have him back on board in a jiffy.''

''But there are sharks in these waters. We saw

two big ones following the ship this afternoon. Oh, Harry, we never should have brought him on this cruise. If anything has happened to him, we are to blame, because we insisted that he and Ramona should see the world together, before marrying.''

''No, it is not your fault. It is mine.''

It was Ramona who startled the group by this sudden assertion.

''Why, Ramona! What do you mean, dear?'' the *doña* asked.

''We quarreled,'' she said. ''I told him I would leave him—never wanted to see him again. And now he has gone—gone to his death.''

She turned suddenly and flung herself sobbing into the arms of her foster mother.

Standing a few feet away from the group, mumbling his quid of betel, Babu Chandra Kumar smiled knowingly and spat into the water.

The yacht came about with engines throbbing, then slowly cruised back over her former course, her searchlight sweeping the waves. A lifeboat was unshipped and swung out on its davits, ready to be lowered at a moment's notice. Men stood along the rails with life preservers, the lines coiled and ready.

The five who stood together on the foredeck moved to the bow, where they anxiously scanned the water, the *doña* striving to reassure the sobbing girl, and Trevor supporting his half fainting wife.

Unnoticed by the others, the babu crossed the deck to the opposite rail as the ship came about. But instead of futilely gazing at the water ahead, he kept his eyes on the sampan, which was now nosing out toward the yacht.

Aided by the offshore breeze, the little sailing vessel made rapid progress in the direction of the yacht. And because of the reduced speed of the latter vessel, it had no difficulty in overhauling it.

As it drew near, the babu made out a turbaned figure in white standing at the rail. Instantly he ran, shouting, toward the little group in the bow.

"The maharaja comes!" he cried. "It is fishing boat of my master. Perhaps he can help us."

"The maharaja!" exclaimed Trevor. "How do you know, *babuji*?"

"That is his fishing vessel. And he is aboard."

"That's right. He told us at Singapore that he would be fishing in these waters."

"Ahoy the yacht," came a call from the sampan. "Anything wrong?"

Trevor cupped his hands as the sampan drew closer.

"My son is overboard, Maharaja," he shouted. "We are looking for him."

"Shocking! I'll help you search."

The two vessels cruised about in the vicinity until past midnight. Then both hove to, side by side, and the Maharaja of Varuda came aboard the yacht. He was slight and slender, with an iron-gray beard, a thin, hooked nose, curved like the blade of a scimitar, and small beady eyes that accentuated his hawk-like expression. Save for his jeweled turban, his dress was English, even to a beribboned monocle. Two handsome Hindu boys in their native garb followed him over the rail.

The maharaja bent low over the hand of the heart-broken Georgia Trevor. "Madame, I am devastated," he said. "But do not give up hope. Your son may have reached the shore. I believe you told me at Singapore that he was a strong swimmer."

"But the sharks! What could he do against those monsters?"

"They are not so numerous as you might think. As soon as it grows light enough I'll have my men search the shore line for some sign of him."

"You are very kind, *maharaja sahib,* but I fear it will be useless."

The maharaja greeted each of the others in turn, then addressed Harry Trevor.

"We have done all that is humanly possible tonight," he said. "I suggest that you drop anchor here, and rest in your cabins until morning. In the meantime, I will go ashore and organize my men for a search of the beach as soon as the sun rises."

"That's good of you, Maharaja," said Trevor, "but I can't remain here inactive. I'll go ashore with you."

"I, too," replied Don Francesco. "It is maddening to think of waiting here and doing nothing."

"Come ashore if you like, gentlemen. You will be welcome at my camp."

"May humble servant come also, your highness?" asked Babu Chandra Kumar. "Should like to help, if your highness will permit." He paused to snivel and brush away a tear. "I loved young *sahib* like son and had counted on exalted privilege of escorting him about Calcutta."

"You will probably be in the way," said the maharaja, with a disdainful glance at the babu's obese figure, "but come, anyway, since the *sahibs* will not have any immediate use for your services as a guide. And bring your man. I have heard that he is a good *shikari,* and we may need men who are expert at trailing."

"Kupta is very great *shikari,* your highness. Can follow trail like hound."

THE MAHARAJAH

Save for the half dozen men who stood guard, the camp of the maharaja was asleep when the party went ashore. Against the dark background of the jungle loomed a score of huge, slate-gray shapes—elephants. A few had lain down, but most of them stood, shifting their huge bulks from side to side, clanking their leg-chains and switching grass up over their backs.

The maharaja waved the babu and his servant to quarters among the mahouts. Trevor and Don Francesco were ushered to the richly carpeted and cushioned tent of his highness. Servants brought assorted liquors, soda, ice, cigarettes and cigars.

"Make yourselves comfortable, gentlemen," said the maharaja. "My tent is your tent and my servants are your servants. I must ask you to excuse me for a few moments. The elephants are restless, and I wish to inspect them. Only last night my most valuable elephant ran away, and Angad, her mahout, who went after her, has not returned.

"We may have urgent need for the others in the morning, so it would be embarrassing to have any more break away tonight."

"You mean—"began Trevor.

"I mean," replied the maharaja, "that if we find your son has made his way ashore, it is possible that we may have to do some dangerous jungle traveling to overtake him. My trackers will find him eventually, of course, but it will be the elephants that will carry us and our supplies. There is no safer, surer mode of jungle transportation."

He took a cigarette which one servant proffered in a jeweled box, permitted the other to light it, and, turning, left the tent. But he did not go to the elephant lines. Instead, he walked into a near-by tent where Babu Chandra Kumar sat alone.

The babu rose and made obeisance.

"You are sure there is no one within hearing?" asked the maharaja, glaring through his monocle.

"Am positive, your highness," replied the babu. "Kupta is already asleep, and none other except guards are stirring."

"Good. And now your report."

"The red-headed one is dead," said the babu. "Many leagues back Kupta slew him and threw him to sharks, while humble servant held attention of man in wheelhouse. Everything was done according to your highness' orders."

"And you secured one of his handkerchiefs?"

"Yes, highness."

The babu produced a silk handkerchief in one corner of which were the initials "J. T."

"Splendid! Put it away until I signal you to produce it. But remember, it must be torn and bedraggled."

"Humble servant will see to that, highness."

"And now I have another task for you to perform. Take Sarkar, the mahout, who is about the size of the young red-headed *sahib,* and row along the shore to the southeast for a quarter of a mile. Then let him walk ashore barefooted on the sandy beach and make his way back to camp through the jungle, being careful to conceal his trail after he leaves the beach."

"Your highness, being so generous, will no doubt recall that humble servant is poor man with large family in Howrah," said the babu.

"I will remember," replied the maharaja. "Already you have had a thousand rupees to divide with Kupta. Here is another thousand for serving me faithfully until we reach my palace. But all this is mere expense money. Once the little dark-eyed beauty is safely delivered into the hands of my priests, no suspicion attaching to me for her disappearance, a lakh of rupees shall be yours. And if you show sufficient cleverness and aptitude it may be that I will make you my *deewan* for life."

"Your highness is most generous, indeed," replied the babu, bowing profoundly as the maharaja took his leave. But once the potentate had gone, he stuffed a quid of betel into his fat cheek and computed his possible profits for the journey. Already he had done Kupta out of four hundred rupees which were supposed to have gone to him for his assassin's work on the boat. The mahout, he felt sure, would do his part and keep silent for ten rupees. And for another fifty Kupta would willingly lead the assemblage through the jungle toward the maharaja's palace, while making it appear that he was trailing Jan.

With a betel-stained smile, Chandra Kumar arose ponderously and went out toward the elephant lines, where Sarkar, the mahout, was sleeping.

CHAPTER III

MAN-EATERS

As he leaned morosely over the rail, gazing at the distant jungle, Jan's first intimation of danger was when something crashed down on his head with stunning force. Things grew blurred and indistinct, and there was a strange weakness in his arms and legs. He sank to the rail. Then, though he felt himself being lifted and heaved overboard, he was unable to make the slightest resistance—could not even turn his head to look at his unknown enemy.

He splashed into the waves head-on, and went down through a seething maelstrom of black waters. The shock of falling into the water partly revived him, and he struggled feebly to reach the surface, meanwhile instinctively holding his breath.

Presently, when it seemed that his aching lungs were about to collapse, his head emerged into the air. He took a deep breath, shook the water fom his eyes, and looked about him. The yacht was already more than a quarter of a mile away, and rapidly widening the distance between them. To shout, he knew, would be useless. At his right, not more than a mile distant, stretched a white ribbon of moonlit beach, and behind it the mysterious jungle which had so intrigued him. He kicked off his oxfords and removed his mess jacket. Once free of these impediments, he set out for the shore with long, steady strokes.

His head cleared rapidly as he made his way shoreward, and it occurred to him to wonder who had made this attempt on his life. On all the yacht, so far as he knew, he had not one single enemy. The captain and crew had all been friendly throughout the voyage. The babu and his servant, both of whom had graciously been lent to his father in Singapore by the maharaja, so the former might act as their dragoman in Calcutta, had been especially obsequious. His father and mother were ruled out, of course. Nor could the *don* and *doña* have any possible reason for wanting to do away with him. But he had quarreled with Ramona. She had told him their engagement was over—that she never wanted to see him again.

Had Jan been brought up among men, he would have gained sufficient knowledge of human nature to be positive that the gentle Ramona, despite her tropical temper, would never attempt to kill him. But he had lived the greater part of his life in the jungle, and jungle codes were still a part of his nature.

Ramona had told him that she hated him—had been the only one on the yacht who had shown any open hostility toward him. And so he concluded that she had suited her actions to her words and had deliberately attempted to murder him. It was thus that any jungle creature would do—that he himself would do without compunction upon sufficent provocation.

The conviction brought him a greater sadness that he had ever known, for Ramona had come to mean more to him than life itself. And so, though he continued to swim onward with listless, automatic strokes, his heart was so heavy within him that he did not care whether he lived or died.

But in times of emergency, instinct is often stronger than reason or emotion. And so when Jan, chancing to look back, caught the glint of moonlight on a sail-like fin that was coming rapidly toward him, the instinct to live took command of him. He doubled, trebled, and presently quadrupled his former speed toward the shore. But each time, on glancing back, he saw that the dread killer of the sea was rapidly shortening the distance between them.

Presently, with the shore not more than a hundred yards distant, and the shark less than twenty feet behind him, he realized that his pursuer would be upon him before he could cover a third of the remaining distance. Ripping off his shirt, he flung it back over his head. It distracted the attention of the killer for a moment, during which the monster seized it and tore it to shreds in its razor sharp teeth. And during that moment, Jan gained a few feet. Taking his pocketknife from his trousers and placing it in his mouth, he wriggled free. Then, when the shark was a scant ten feet behind him, he tossed the sodden garment between them.

Again the attention of the monster was distracted, and again Jan made a gain of a few feet. But the fish soon relinquished its tasteless morsel, and Jan, despite the fact that he was now making better progress than before, found himself being rapidly overhauled. Further flight, he saw, was futile, for it could only end in his being seized from behind in those cruel jaws. And with only a small pocketknife for a weapon, to turn and fight seemed equally hopeless.

But turn he did, after opening the blade and gripping the knife once more between his teeth. The monster was so close now that he could see it distinctly in the moonlight. It was a large hammerhead, fully fifteen feet in length, the most grotesque and one of the most dangerous of all the sharks that inhabit the Indian Ocean.

Seeing its toothsome quarry motionless, and apparently helpless, the shark plunged forward, opening its gleaming jaws to seize its prey. But when the flat snout was within two feet of him, Jan suddenly reached out with both hands and seized the two strange projections on each side of the monster's head, which gave it its name.

Puzzled by such unexpected tactics, the shark plunged onward, still trying to reach its intended victim. But it only succeeded in pushing the jungle man further toward the shore with each snapping lunge. Presently, after it had advanced about fifty feet in this fashion, it tired of such fruitless endeavors, shook its head free of those gripping hands, and backed away. Jan seized the opportunity to retreat, swimming backward and still keeping a sharp watch on his enemy.

It was well that he did so, for in a moment the shark darted forward once more, this time with lightning speed. Again Jan thrust out his hands, but this time, instead of merely employing them to keep his attacker away from him, he tightly gripped the two projections, and bearing down upon them, somersaulted over onto the creature's back and clamped his legs beneath the body just in front of the pectoral fins.

The monster instantly plunged under water, turning over and over to dislodge him. But he held his breath, and shifting his hold to the gill slits, turned his body so he was facing forward. Then he again clamped his legs around the body, and taking his pocketknife from between his teeth, tried to force the puny blade into the creature's brain. The thick skull, however, baffled him, so he shifted his attack to the eyes, which were situated at the extremities of the hammer-like projections. He successfully gouged out first one eye, then the other, while he maintained his precarious seat by means of his body-scissors and the gill slits. Then he carefully felt for and cut the jaw hinges on each side, rendering the shark incapable of seizing its prey.

This done, he kicked himself free of the monster, and swam for the surface, where he filled his aching lungs again and again. The shark broke water about thirty feet behind him a moment later, and he saw, to his consternation, that two more man-eaters were converging toward him, evidently attracted by the sounds of the struggle or the scent of animal blood.

The shore was now but a hundred feet distant, and without a moment's hesitation, Jan turned and swam for it at top speed. But to his surprise and consternation, the maimed shark followed him as swiftly and unerringly as if it had not lost its sight— evidently by scent or sound, or perhaps both. In

the meantime, the other two sharks came in from
both sides with tremendous speed.

Jan covered fifty feet, and was again forced to
turn and prepare to fight, but with three enemies
this time instead of one. They came so swiftly that
the last fifty feet might have been a mile, so far as
his hope of escape was concerned. It was the most
desperate situation in which he had ever found
himself—desperate to the point of hopelessness. For
what could he do against three such mighty enemies
in their own element?

The two oncoming sharks drew up beside their
maimed companion, now less than five feet from
Jan. Then an astounding thing happened. For, instead of assisting in the pursuit, both simultaneously
attacked the wounded hammerhead. In an instant
there was a terrific struggle, a mighty threshing in
the boiling, foaming water.

But Jan did not wait to see the outcome. Instead,
he turned and once more struck out for the beach.
A dozen powerful strokes, and he felt the sloping
sand beneath his feet. He rose and ran splashing
through the shallows. Not until dry sand was beneath him did he turn. The three contestants had
disappeared, leaving only a few bubbles to mark
the point of the struggle.

By this time, the yacht was only a speck of
light upon the horizon. Jan stood resting from his
exertions and watched it until it disappeared from
view. Then he turned toward the dark, mysterious
jungle behind him. The breeze carried the same
scents and sounds that had attracted him when on
the yacht. But the scents were much stronger, and the
sounds much plainer, now.

For some time he stood there listening—sniffing

the air. There remained to him only a few shreds of his underclothing, which had been torn in his struggle with the shark, and his pocketknife. He skillfully twisted the shreds into a G string and with his wet socks made a small pouch at one side for the knife. Then he melted silently into the shadowy depths of the forest.

Though his tread was as noiseless as that of any jungle cat, and his eyes, ears and nostrils were keenly alert for danger from the denizens of this unknown wilderness, the jungle bred Jan made his way forward as fearlessly as any man born and reared in civilization would walk the streets of his native city.

Presently, there came to him a powerful, unmistakable cat scent from close behind him, brought to him by a sudden shifting of the breeze. Instantly, he knew that a big feline of a breed new and strange to him was stalking him, and near enough for the charge. He turned, and caught the gleam of a great blinking pair of eyes.

Knowing itself discovered, the beast let out a roar, and charged. But with an agility which equaled that of the great cat, Jan sprang for the nearest tree, and swung himself into the lower branches just in time to escape the raking claws beneath him. He quickly made his way upward, but paused in his climb when a low growl suddenly came from the branch above him, accompanied by a new cat scent and the scratching of nails on bark, which told him that another large feline was descending to attack him.

Instantly he swung outward as far as he dared, on the limb upon which he was perched. Then, in a mottled patch of moonlight he caught sight of the descending brute against the trunk of the tree. It was jet black, with great yellow eyes, and about the size of a cougar.

On the ground below him the moonlight revealed the striped body of a cat that was larger, but no more dangerous to an unarmed man, than the one that was descending toward him. And while the tiger gazed upward, snarling and expectantly licking its chops, the black fury dropped lightly to the limb on which Jan was balanced, and with ears laid back and tail lashing the leaves, crouched for a spring.

CHAPTER IV

A FALSE TRAIL

After the maharaja left the babu he did not inspect the elephant lines. Instead, he returned to his own tent where Trevor paced nervously back and forth, while Don Francesco sat in his chair and puffed violently at his slender, black cigar. Adjusting his monocle, the potentate walked to the table, sat down, and selected a cigarette which a servant quickly lighted for him.

"Rotten go, this," he remarked.

"There's nothing more we can do until morning. Now if it had only happened in the day time we could be doing things. But this beastly waiting jangles one's nerves."

"It does that," Trevor agreed explosively. "Enough to drive a man nuts."

"Quite. But you mustn't let it get you. Come. Sit down and let me be your doctor. I prescribe a spot of brandy."

"His highness is right, *amigo*," said Don

Francesco. "Worry can accomplish nothing. Constructive thinking and planning may help."

"Of course," replied Trevor, coming to the table. "I am a fool to get jittery. What's needed is constructive planning, and action."

Waving his servants away, the maharaja poured brandy for his guests.

Trevor tasted his drink and reached for a cigarette.

"Do you think, maharaja, that we will be able to find Jan in the morning—that is if he's still alive?"

"There is a strong possibility that we may," was the reply. "We can at least assure ourselves as to whether or not he has come ashore."

"How?"

"For several miles in both directions the beach is of soft sand. My trackers will easily be able to discern whether or not a man has come ashore."

"Right. But suppose he has gone on into the jungle. I have an idea that is the thing he is most likely to do. He grew up in the jungle, you know, and we all noticed that he seemed strangely attracted by this one the moment we came within sight of it."

"In that case," said the maharaja, "we must follow his trail until we can come up with him. My shikaris will be able to find him eventually, but it may take time."

"There is a possibility that we may be stuck here for days, weeks—even months."

"That is true," said the maharaja. "When we met in Singapore I did myself the honor of inviting you and your party to visit me. You declined then, because of your haste to get back to your affairs in America. However, since this matter has come up, it may be that you will change your mind. I flatter myself with the hope that you will, and place all the resources of my little kingdom at your disposal.''

"You are most kind, *maharaja sahib*," said Trevor. "I declined before because of urgent business at home. But there can be no more urgent business for me than the finding of my son. If a long search for him should be indicated by what we find in the morning, I will gladly avail myself of your kind invitation."

Morning dawned at last, and the camp was instantly astir with feverish activity. The maharaja divided his men into two parties to search the beach, one to go northwest, the other southeast. At his suggestion, Don Francesco accompanied the first party while he and Trevor went with the other.

At the head of this latter group of searchers waddled the fat babu, accompanied by Kupta the hillman.

Presently, when they had proceeded about a half a mile along the shore, the babu threw up his hands.

"Stop!" he cried. "Freshly tracks are here coming up out of the water."

Trevor sprang forward.

"Where?" he cried.

But a moment later, he saw them himself. The tracks of barefeet leading from the water's edge toward the jungle.

"Jan wore shoes," he said, "but he would have kicked them off in the water. Probably got rid of his socks, also." He turned to the maharaja. "Do you think it possible that any one else might have swum ashore here?"

"Hardly. No one left my little boat, and so far as we are aware, nobody but your son left the yacht. No one with any knowledge of these waters would be likely to try it from any other craft because of the danger from sharks. Your son, it seems, has escaped them by some miracle.

"Then you are reasonably certain these are Jan's tracks."

"Wait. Let us make sure." He called the babu. "Have your hillman inspect the tracks and tell us what sort of person made them," he ordered. Then he turned once more to Trevor. "The things these hillmen can tell from a few marks in the sand are uncanny," he said.

At Chandra Kumar's command, Kupta bent over the tracks. There followed a swift muttering in Urdu.

"*Shikari* says these are not tracks of Indian man, but of young and strongly *sahib*," the babu announced.

"That settles it," said the maharaja. "Take two men and go with him. Follow the trail into the jungle. In a half hour, send a man back to camp with news of what you have found on the trail. And in another half hour stop and wait for us, sending the second man to lead us to you. We will return for the elephants, and to pack."

When Trevor and the maharaja got back to the camp, they found that the ladies had already arrived there in one of the yacht's lifeboats, piloted by Officer Nelson. The eyes of all three showed the effect of a tearful, sleepless night.

"Have you learned anything?" all wanted to know in unison.

"Something that gives me great hope," Trevor replied. "Tracks leading into the jungle. We believe that Jan is alive and somewhere nearby."

"Alone and unarmed!" exclaimed Georgia Trevor. "What can he do? He will starve, or be devoured by wild beasts."

"I doubt that he will do either," said her husband. "Jan didn't manage to survive in the South American jungle for many years without learning a thing or two. The boy will be able to take care of himself. And we may find him any time now. An expert tracker is already on his trail, and we will follow as soon as the elephants are loaded."

"You will follow? But what of us? Are we to be left behind to—to die of suspense?"

"I have two large howdahs in addition to the pad elephants," said the maharaja. "There will be ample room for all if you care to come with us."

"But will it not be dangerous for the ladies?" asked Don Francesco.

"Not at all," replied the potentate. "The back of a docile and intelligent elephant is the safest place for any one in the jungle."

In less than a half hour the caravan was loaded and on its way into the jungle. The second man, who had come from Kupta and the babu, led the way. In the first howdah rode the maharaja with Trevor, Don Francesco, and a servant to take charge of the rifles. In the second rode the three ladies. Behind them came the loaded pad elephants. And strung out in two files, one on each side, walked the maharaja's retainers, armed with spears and large jungle knives.

An hour's ride brought them to the bank of a small stream. And here, squatting at their ease in the dense shade of a deodar tree, they found the babu and Kupta, mumbling their betel and expectorating red juice at such unfortunate insects as chanced to wander within range.

At the sight of the maharaja's elephant, the babu hoisted himself ponderously to his feet, and the hillman sprang lightly up beside him. Then both salaamed.

"Proceed on the trail, *babuji*," ordered the maharaja, "and see to it that your hillman does not lead us astray."

"He will not lose trail, your highness," the babu replied. "Kupta is very expertly *shikari*."

Taking a rusty looking old umbrella which Sarkar, the mahout, had brought him from his private kit, he raised it over his head and waddled off behind the wiry hillman.

They followed the stream for some distance, then crossed at a shallow ford which seemed to have been used extensively both by domestic and jungle animals. The bank, which had been flattened out for more than a hundred feet on both sides of the stream, was indented with the tracks of elephants, deer, buffalo, horses and other lesser herbivores, and in the soft mud at the water's edge, Trevor saw the pugs of tigers and leopards. Obviously it was an old game trail which had come to be frequently utilized by man.

Having crossed the ford, Kupta circled for a time, then struck off in a northerly direction. The babu lumbered heavily after him, grunting, wheezing, and using the greasy end of his turban from time to time to mop the streaming perspiration from his eyes.

Trevor, to whom jungle travel was no novelty, noticed that they crossed and recrossed the well-marked game trail they had passed at the ford, but never stayed upon it for any great length of time. He concluded, from this, that Jan was following the trail, possibly in the hope of reaching civilization, or perhaps for the more primitive and necessary purpose of making a kill.

At noon they paused at a little pool, fed by a limpid spring which trickled down from the rocky hillside. Scarcely had the elephants paused to discharge their passengers, when the babu, who had climbed up beside the spring for a drink of water, came rushing toward them, waving a torn, sodden handkerchief and shouting shrilly.

"Highness, *Sahibs*! *Memsahibs*! Have found most importantly clue! See! See!"

"What is it, *babuji*? Let me see," said Trevor, who had been the first to dismount.

With the important air of one who has made a momentous discovery, Chandra Kumar handed him the handkerchief.

"Look at initials—in corner," puffed the babu.

"'J. T.,' by the gods!" exclaimed Trevor. "It's Jan's, all right."

The ragged bit of cloth was quickly passed from hand to hand as the others crowded around, and as quickly identified. The maharaja was the last to examine it. He squinted at it through his monocle for a moment. Then he turned to Georgia Trevor.

"You are positive that this is your son's handkerchief?" he asked.

"Positive."

"Then it is time for us to crystallize our plans. We have found that he is traveling swiftly to the northward. If he continues, he will soon be in my territory, Varuda, and my palace at Varudapur will be an ideal base from which to conduct our search. I therefore suggest that we make camp here, and send two pad elephants back to the coast for any baggage you may wish to bring with you, instructing the commander of your yacht to take it to Calcutta and there await further orders. In the meantime, I will send the babu and the *shikari* forward on the trail, to learn whither it leads, and to make inquiry as to whether or not any natives they may encounter have seen your son."

Georgia Trevor turned to her husband.

"What do you think, Harry?"

"A splendid plan," he replied. "We accept your suggestion and invitation, maharaja, with pleasure and with gratitude."

The potentate included all five of his guests with a courtly bow. "My house will be most signally honored," he said.

Then he turned, clapped his hands, and issued a few swift orders. In a few moments the elephants were relieved of their loads, and a village of tents grew as if by magic. There was a large tent for the three ladies, another for Trevor and Don Francesco, and a third for the maharaja. All three were sumptuously and lavishly furnished with thick rugs, divans with spring mattresses, silken cushions, and embroidered hangings.

As soon as the two pad elephants had been dispatched, the maharaja retired to his tent and sent for the babu. A few moments later, as Chandra Kumar wheezed in past the ornate curtains, the potentate dismissed his two servants. Then he beckoned the babu to him, and spoke softly in Bengali.

"The first part of our plan is accomplished," he said. "The tracks of Sarkar deceived them, and the handkerchief proved most convincing. But there yet remains much to be done. What of Zafarulla Khan and his Pathan cutthroats? Are you sure they are encamped near here, and that you will be able to find them?"

"Those horse-stealing malefactors would camp where I bade them until the British leave India, for a chance to win the princely sum which your highness has promised them," he replied.

"Very well. Here are the five thousand rupees which you are to pay them. And ten thousand more await them when they deliver the girl to my priests. Now here is the plan in full, and it must be carried out to the letter or we will all be ruined."

His voice dropped to a whisper, and the babu nodded and grunted from time to time, to show that he understood.

Shortly thereafter Chandra Kumar rode away to the northward on a small pad elephant, guided by Sarkar, the mahout, with Kupta ranging before them as if following a trail.

CHAPTER V

JUNGLE TRAGEDY

Unarmed, and out on the end of the limb, with the black leopard ready to spring upon him, while the tiger waited expectantly below, Jan realized that he was in grave danger. Yet he sat there calmly enough—waiting. Suddenly the leopard sprang. And with equal quickness, the jungle man dropped from his perch, swinging by his hands.

The tiger roared and leaped upward at sight of the man dangling so temptingly above him. The leopard, unable to check its impetus, turned in midair and tried to grasp the end of the limb. But Jan's sudden drop had pulled it down out of reach, and the black feline, now squalling with fear, hurtled downward, straight into the waiting claws of the tiger.

Jan once more swung lightly up on the limb, to watch the scrimmage going on in the little moonlit glade below him. He had expected to see the leopard instantly killed, and was therefore surprised to see that it was giving an excellent account of itself, falling on its back and using its fearful hind claws for defense each time it was attacked, while the jungle resounded with its spitting and caterwauling, mingled with the snarls and deep-throated roars of the tiger.

But, though he would have enjoyed seeing the conclusion of this jungle battle, it suddenly came to him that this was his golden opportunity for making good his escape. So he swung away through the interlaced branches and vines as easily as any arboreal ape—and far more swiftly. In a few moments all sounds of the battle died behind him, and the normal night cries of the smaller jungle inhabitants, which fear had stilled in the battle area, were resumed.

For mile after mile he swung along with tireless, effortless ease. And many and varied were the jungle scenes that unfolded beneath him. Once he passed quite near to a herd of elephants, feeding —great ponderous hulks in the moonlight, tearing off branches with their sinuous trunks and munching the leaves and twigs. Presently one of them trumpeted, and he identified the sound he had heard from the yacht.

Farther on he disturbed a tribe of rhesus monkeys in their leafy dormitory, and departed, followed by their chattered imprecations. Later, a skulking leopard passed beneath him, its spots showing plainly in the moonlight, reminding him of the jaguars of his South American jungle.

Presently he came to a large tree in which a pair of peafowls roosted. The hen roused at his

approach and flapped swiftly away through the jungle. But the cock awoke too late. He grasped it by the neck, took out his pocketknife, and in a few moments was feasting on its raw, warm flesh. Again he was reminded of his native jungle, and of the many curassows he had eaten in this same manner.

Having satisfied his hunger, he swung off once more, looking for water to quench his thirst. Presently he reached a tree that overhung a small stream. He was about to descend when a huge striped form slunk out of the shadows beneath him. The tiger waded into the stream up to its sagging belly and stood their lapping the water.

Presently it lay down, wallowing in the shallows. Weary of waiting, Jan presently grew sleepy. He decided to defer his drink until the morrow, so searched out a convenient crotch, curled up, and was soon asleep.

The jungle man was awakened by a shaft of orange gold sunlight which, penetrating his leafy canopy, struck him full in the face. He arose, stretched, and looked down at the scene beneath him. The tiger was gone, but its huge pugs were plainly visible in the soft gravelly bank.

Thirsty as he was, Jan swung through the neighboring trees and made a careful survey of all the nearby thickets before he descended. The water was warm, but clear and sweet, and he noticed that a little farther out there were flat rocks in the stream bed. This gave him an idea; so, after he had satisfied his thirst, he waded out into the stream and looked about until he had found a hard flinty stone which roughly resembled a double-bitted ax head. Deftly he chipped away at it until he had two ragged cutting edges and a groove down the center on both sides.

This done, he cut a straight limb from an iron-wood tree, shaped it into a stout haft with his knife, and after splitting one end, bound the head in place with strips of tough fibrous bark torn from a vine.

When his work was finished the sun had passed the meridian, but he had a stone ax as good as had ever been wielded by neanderthal man. More strips of bark, plaited together, formed a shoulder strap from which he slung his heavy weapon. And primitive though it was, it gave him a feeling of confidence, for he knew that sooner or later he must fight it out with the great carnivores of this jungle, and the weapon would help to counterbalance their superiority of tooth and claw. Indeed, he was more than a little anxious to try conclusions with the next tiger or leopard that might come this way, as he always preferred fight to flight, where there was anything approaching an equal chance.

Jan had been so engrossed in the making of his weapon that he had forgotten all about food. Now, however, his empty stomach began to remind him of his negligence. And the sight of a school of fish moving lazily through the shallows quickened his appetite. In a clump of bamboo nearby he found a pole that had been broken off by the passage of some heavy animal, and was quite well seasoned. After trimming off the branches and cutting it down to the required length, he split the segment at one end into four pieces, which he held apart by means of crossed sticks bound with bits of bark. After sharpening the four ends he took his fishing spear to the stream and soon had three fat fish gasping on the bank.

He crouched beside his catch, ate them raw, and after a long, satisfying drink from the stream, proceeded along the bank. He had followed the stream for some distance when, upon rounding a sharp turn, he suddenly came face to face with a huge, leather-armored beast with a horn on its snout, wallowing in the mud.

With an angry snort, the rhinoceros scrambled to its feet and charged. Jan hurled his spear straight at the monster's lowered head and, turning, sprang up the bank. He caught hold of a stout vine and scrambled up hand over hand, just in time to escape the earth-shaking charge. The bamboo spear, instead of checking the brute, had only served to infuriate it, and it rooted angrily at the base of the tree, gouging out great chunks of bark.

But the jungle man did not remain in that tree. Instead, he resumed his journey, keeping to the trees and vines which overhung the stream. He traveled thus until the sun hung low on the horizon. Then there came to his sensitive nostrils the pungent smell of wood smoke, and something else—the strong scent of tiger.

Cautiously, soundlessly, he swung onward, and in a moment saw the source of the smoke. A brown man, naked save for the dhoti about his loins, and his turban, was bending over a small cooking fire. With him was a brown boy similarly attired, who had just brought up an armful of wood and was starting out for another. Jan saw that the man was stirring something in a small kettle over the fire, that a large, double curved knife hung at his side, and a long spear lay near at hand. A few feet from the fire was a crude shelter of bamboo thatched with leaves.

The boy walked straight toward the tree in which the jungle man was perched. In his right hand he carried a knife, double-curved like that of the man, but smaller, and with this, as he came beneath the tree, he began cutting bits of underbrush for firewood.

At this instant Jan discovered the source of the cat scent. A huge tigress, taking advantage of every bit of available cover, was noiselessly stalking the boy—was at that moment not thirty feet from him.

Swiftly the jungle man dropped from limb to limb. To shout a warning to the boy he knew would be useless. The great cat would have him before he could run ten feet. As Jan reached the lowermost limb the tigress uttered a rumbling growl and charged. The boy stood rooted to his tracks by terror.

Lightly the jungle man dropped between the charging feline and its prey, his stone ax ready for action. The tigress paused for an instant, then seeing that only a man faced her, charged forward with renewed fury.

Jan waited until she reared up on her hind legs to seize him. Then he swung his stone ax with a circular motion that caught the brute a terrific blow on the side of the head. The jagged stone struck between eye and ear with such force that the eye popped out of its socket and the beast was bowled over on her right side.

Roaring with fury, the tigress scrambled to her feet and renewed the attack. This time Jan clouted her on the other side of the head, again knocking her off balance and rolling her over and over. Half dazed, she lay still for a moment, and the jungle man rushed in for the finishing stroke. But the tigress was far from dead, though she was now reduced to fighting defensively.

Throwing herself first on one side, then the other, she succeeded in warding off the blows from her head and body with her raking claws, and also in inflicting several deep gashes upon her enemy.

At this juncture Jan heard a shriek from the direction of the camp. From the tail of his eye he saw beside the fire the naked brown man struggling in the jaws of a tiger, evidently the mate of the beast he was fighting. The tigress, however, was still very much alive, so much so that the jungle man dared not turn away or relinquish the advantage he had gained. To do so would have meant almost certain death.

When next he was able to look toward the camp fire he saw that it was deserted. A moment later a childish voice that shook with terror sounded behind him.

"I have brought my father's spear for you, *sahib*."

"Give it to me."

The spear was thrust around in front of him.

Jan dropped the ax and seized it. In a moment he had plunged the long steel blade through the heart of the snarling carnivore, pinning her to the ground; and in another, she had relaxed in death.

The jungle man turned and looked at the small brown boy, who stood with tears coursing down his cheeks.

"O great *shikari*, O mighty hunter," he quavered. "The other *bagh* has carried off my father. Perhaps he still lives. Will you kill it also, and save him for me?"

"I'll try," Jan promised.

He wrenched the spear from the carcass of the fallen tigress, took up his stone ax, and slung it from the carry strap. Then he hurried to the camp fire. The trail left by the man-eater was plain enough. The brute had bounded away with great twenty-foot leaps, carrying the man as easily as a cat carries a rat. Occasional gouts of blood from the wounded man spattered the trail.

Jan set out, following at a swift, tireless trot. The little brown boy clung close at his heels. Soon the track showed that the tiger had slowed down to a trot. The huge pugs were comparatively close together, and there were narrow lines left by the dragging feet of its victim.

The trail paralleled the little stream and suddenly brought them to its confluence with a broader one—a small river. Here the pugs led straight down to the water's edge and ended in the shallows.

"The *bagh* has swum the river," said the boy.

"We will swim after him," Jan replied.

"But there are muggers—big ones. They would eat us."

The lad pointed to where several ugly crocodile snouts projected above the surface.

Jan barely glanced at them. Then he looked across the narrow river. The farther bank was plainly visible, and there were no tiger pugs on it. Yet the tiger could not have climbed up that bank without leaving a plain trail. Perhaps it had only swum up or down stream for a short distance, then come out on the same side. Jan searched the bank for a half mile in both directions, but found no tracks.

"Maybe the muggers got both," hazarded the boy.

"In any event, it will be too late to save your father if we find him now," Jan replied.

"But I would save him from being eaten, *sahib*, that I may perform the true duties of an eldest son."

"And what may that be?"

"To burn his body and cast his ashes into the Ganges."

Jan shook his head uncomprehendingly. He could not understand the sense of risking one's life to save a dead body, only to burn it immediately afterward. Yet, somehow, he liked this black-eyed, brown-skinned lad.

"We will cross the river," he announced.

Some distance upstream he had noticed a place where the leafy vault of trees and vines came almost together above the stream. He led the way to this point, the boy following.

"Get up on my back," he ordered, "and hold the spear."

The lad did as he was bidden, and Jan swarmed effortlessly up a thick vine with his light burden. He soon found a stout projecting limb that suited his purpose, and walked out on it until he stood high above the middle of the stream.

"Hang on," he cried. Then he leaped as a diver leaps from a springboard. The brown boy gasped, but clung tightly as they hurtled dizzily through space.

Jan caught a limb of the opposite tree some ten feet lower down, and clung. It sagged dangerously, and a huge mugger below them opened its jaws as if in pleasant anticipation. But the limb held, and in a moment more the two stood safely on the bank. Jan took the spear.

"Now we will look for the *bagh*," he said.

They walked back along the bank, and presently the jungle man saw the trail which had escaped him before.

The tiger had swum straight across, but instead of going up the bank had pulled itself up on the trunk of a tree undermined by the current which sagged out horizontally only a foot above the water.

The trail led straight back through the trees, over a low hill, and into a patch of tall jungle grass. Jan went warily through that grass, his spear ready poised in his hand for instant action. It was an ideal hiding place for any animal, but most especially for a tiger, whose stripes so perfectly simulated its pattern of light and shadow.

The path wound through the grass for a short distance. Then they suddenly came upon the trampled, blood-soaked spot where the tiger had devoured its kill. The signs were unmistakable. And all that the beast had left consisted of a dedraggled turban, some chewed bits of loin cloth, and the long, double-curved knife which the deceased had worn at his waist, attached to the ragged stubs of what had once been a leather belt.

The boy gathered the grisly tokens into a little pile, then squatted on his heels before them, rocking back and forth and moaning.

Jan watched him for some time in silence. Presently he said: "Come. We have yet to find the *bagh* and slay it."

"It is useless to find the *bagh* now," groaned the boy, "for I cannot perform the funeral rites for my father."

"Why not?" Jan asked. "Since your father is

inside the *bagh*, we will slay the beast and burn it. Thus you may perform the funeral rites for your father and later cast his ashes into the Ganges.''

The lad looked up thoughtfully.

''I do not know that the Brahmins would approve of such a burning,'' he said. ''And yet, it is all that is left to do. So let us look for the *bagh*.'' He picked up the turban and knife, and stood up. The former, he fitted over his own small turban. The latter he extended to Jan. ''Take this *kukrie*,'' he said, ''''since you do not have one. It will be very useful in the jungle.''

Jan accepted the gift with befitting gravity, and set off once more on the trail of the tiger. It wound through the grass for some distance, then led back through the trees toward the river. Soon the cat scent grew very strong, and the jungle man moved forward with the utmost caution. Presently he saw the tiger sprawling in the shallows in a little inlet that connected with the river.

Noiselessly, he raised the heavy spear for the cast. But it was never made. For at that instant, Jan felt a stinging pain in his right forearm. A great, spade-shaped serpent head was clamped upon it. He dropped the spear, and gripping the snake behind the head with his left hand, squeezed it until its jaws loosened. But in the meantime the heavy coils of its enormous body had slithered down from the branch on which they were draped, and were flung, one after another, around his shoulder, as a hawser is thrown over a mooring post. Jan managed to keep his head and body free of those coils, but his right arm and shoulder were imprisoned.

Hearing the struggle so close at hand, the tiger

bounded to its feet. Instantly catching sight of the jungle man, it growled thunderously and charged. Jan made a superhuman effort to wrench his arm and shoulder free from those crushing folds, but he could not loosen the vise-like grip of the reptile.

CHAPTER VI

THE RAID

As soon as the babu had ridden well out of sight of the camp on the pad elephant, he ordered Sarkar, the mahout, to halt the beast, and called Kupta to come and ride with him. Then they started off once more, this time at a swifter pace, and straight for their objective, without any pretense of following a trail.

After a ride of about five miles, they came to a small camp situated in a pleasant grove of trees, through which a clear brook meandered. A short distance from the camp a herd of horses was grazing under the watchful eyes of two mounted and armed Pathans. Swarthy, bearded men lounged about in the shade, smoking and chatting.

As the elephant approached, one of these seized a rifle, sprang to his feet, and shouted a challenge in Pashto.

"Ho, strangers. What do you want?"

"I seek a word with Zafarulla Khan," replied the babu in the same language.

"Then you are Chandra Kumar?"

"In the flesh."

"In very good flesh, I observe," said the Pathan with a sly wink at his comrades, who laughed uproariously as the babu closed his umbrella and clumsily dismounted from his seat on the kneeling elephant.

"Said the crow to the pigeon," replied Chandra Kumar with a bland smile.

Whereupon the laugh was turned against the jester, for he was a very lean and cadaverous man. But like many jesters, he could give with better grace than he could receive.

"Our leader expects you, O father of a pig," he snarled.

"Lead on, my son, and I will follow," retorted the babu, with his same bland smile.

Goaded by the laughter of his comrades at this unexpected retort, the Pathan glared furiously and raised his rifle threateningly, as if he would brain the babu with it.

But the latter stood his ground without a change of countenance, so he turned and strode away, Chandra Kumar waddling after him.

He stopped before one of the tents. "The Bengali has come," he announced. Then he stalked away.

The babu paused at the doorway.

"*Adab Zafarulla Khan,*" he said pleasantly.

"*Adab araz, babuji,*" was the deep voiced reply. "*Bismillah!* Enter, in the name of Allah."

The babu kicked off his slippers, dropped his folded umbrella across them, and stepped inside.

Zafarulla Khan, a perfect giant of a man with a beard dyed flaming red with henna, and a fierce, hawk-like countenance that was seamed with battle scars, sat cross-legged on a blood red Baluchi rug, smoking a hookah. His rifle leaned against a bale of rugs nearby, and his heavy *tulwar* lay beside him. A huge *churdh*, the terrible Afghan knife, kept company with a pair of pearl handled revolvers that were thrust into his sash.

"*Fahdul*," he invited with a wave of his hand. "Be seated."

The babu sat down ponderously and accepted the flexible, ivory bitted stem of the hookah which his host passed to him. Placing it to his lips, he inhaled deeply, making the neroli-scented water bubble noisily in the ornate bowl.

The Pathan clapped his hands, and a beardless boy appeared in the doorway.

"*Shai*," roared Zafarulla Khan.

In a few moments, the boy returned with two small glasses of sweet, syrupy tea. Minutes were consumed in sipping, puffing, and polite inquiries as to the state of each man's health, as well as his family and all his immediate relatives.

This formality concluded, the babu got down to business.

"It is set for tonight," he said.

"It is not set until I give the word," growled Zafarulla Khan. "Where is the money?"

"Here. Count it," Chandra Kurmar tossed a clinking bag between them. "Twenty-five hundred rupees."

"What's that!" roared the Pathan. "*Wallahi!* You were to bring five thousand. The agreement was for ten thousand rupees, one-half down and one-half when the girl is delivered to the priest. Now by my head and beard—''

''Wait.'' The babu checked him with upraised hand, then continued blandly: ''You must have misunderstood. I told you the priest would pay you five thousand when the girl was delivered, and I would pay you half that sum before the raid.''

''You said five thousand, O dog and son of a dog!''

''I distinctly said, one half of that amount.''

''One half of ten thousand!''

''No, of five.''

Zafarulla Khan raged, fumed, blustered and pleaded. He called upon Allah, Mohammed, and all the Moslem saints and prophets to bear him witness. But through it all the babu remained placid and unruffled.

When the storm had somewhat subsided, Chandra Kumar proffered his betel box, but the Pathan struck it from his hand, then drew his *churdh* and fingered the keen blade significantly.

''Do you realize, O unbelieving swine,'' he growled, ''how easy it would be for me to slit your throat, take the money, and leave you here for the hyenas and jackals? The conviction grows upon me that this is what I should do.''

''But it is not what you will do,'' said the babu calmly enough, though he had grown somewhat pale beneath his brown skin.

''And why not?''

''Because if you did, you would have but twenty-five hundred rupees, whereas, for a bloodless raid and a pleasant ride you will have seventy-five hundred. Furthermore, both my master and the

British would hunt you and your men down like mad dogs.''

"Who says the raid will be bloodless and the ride pleasant? It is no light thing to kidnap a *memsahib*. For such a crime the British would hunt a man to the ends of the earth. Better to slit the throat of such as you, take my small gain, and have done with it.''

"But as I have told you, the girl is not a *memsahib*, but an Oriental. You have but to look at her great languorous eyes—her raven hair—''

"Hah! Perhaps I shall keep her for myself.''

"Then you will make the raid?''

"*Ayewah*! But not for this paltry bag of coin—only for the sake of a look at this ravishing beauty.''

The babu chuckled.

"Remember, she is to be turned over unharmed to the priest, if you would collect the five thousand rupees. And no slave girl is worth such a sum. Nor would you chance losing it, were the lovely Nourmahal herself in your power. Your love of gold is too great for that.''

"So *you* think,'' rumbled Zafarulla Khan. "But what of the plans?''

The babu again tendered his betel box, and this time the Pathan helped himself to a quid. Then he reached behind him for a brass cuspidor which he placed on the rug between them.

"The raid is to be staged just after sunset, when it will be light enough to see, yet dark enough so details and disguises will not be seen too clearly.''

"Eh? There will be disguises?''

"I have brought them in a bundle on the elephant, Rajput clothing for all, great black false beards such as the Rajputs wear, and a can of petrol with which beards and clothing may be soaked when you have done with them and are ready to burn them.''

''So! The Rajputs are to take the blame.''

''Why not? It is the only logical disguise.''

''But the only Rajputs in this vicinity are men of the true faith, Moslems like ourselves.''

''Upon whom, then, would you place the blame? And all of the Rajputs in Rissapur are not Muslim. Many have held to the faith of their forefathers.''

''*Billahi*! Rissapur! I begin to smell a mouse in the rice bag! It is said there is no love lost between your Hindu kingling and the Muslim Maharaja of Rissapur.''

''You smell a mouse which does not exist. They are warm friends.''

''Well, perhaps. But I have my doubts. Proceed.''

''You will ride down upon the camp, wearing the Rajput disguises, shouting the Rajput war-cry, and firing your guns into the air.''

''Only to be shot by the *sahibs*.''

''Nay, the *sahibs* will not be in the camp, and the guards will run into the woods at the first sounds of the raid.''

''But I have heard that some of these *memsahibs* can shoot as well as a man.''

''Not these,'' replied the babu. ''Besides, their guns will be loaded with blank cartridges. You will seize the young one and ride off with her, taking care that no harm shall come to her or the others. On arriving at this camp, you will pile your disguises on the ground, pour petrol over them and burn them. Then you will ride on into Rissapur territory.''

"*Subhanullah*! So I thought. The mouse scent again grows strong."

"When you reach the road that leads into the city, you will follow it until you come to the red shrine of Ganesha. Your men will ride on into the city, but you, carrying the girl, will turn off there, and ride alone with her due north until you reach the river. There Thakoor, the priest, will await you with the money."

"Or an ambush to shoot me down."

"Not at all. My master does not wish the plot disclosed, and your men could go to the Maharaja of Rissapur with their grievances if you did not return with the money."

"So they could. Say on."

"When you have received the money you will ride on into Rissapur, pay your men, and order them to leave separately, by various ways, to reunite in any other place you may designate."

The Pathan slapped his thigh.

"*Mashallah*!" he exclaimed. "It is a good scheme, and we are just the men to carry it out. But still the mouse scent lingers. It is whispered that the British Raj would force a union of Varuda and Rissapur, and that the prince who succeeds in winning their favor will rule both. Now if this scandal were brought to the door of the Maharaja of Rissapur—"

"Pure bazaar gossip," the babu interrupted him, rising. "Heed it not, and think no more of superplots which do not exist."

Zafarulla Khan thrust the bag of coins into his sash, and stood up. He towered above the portly babu like a cedar above an olive tree as the two made their way to where the elephant knelt.

With the help of Kupta, the Bengali cast off the ropes which held the bundle of disguises and the means to destroy them, and lowered the bundle to the ground. At a curt command from their leader, two of Zafarulla Khan's men took up the bundle and carried it to his tent.

Then the babu resumed his seat on the pad beside Kupta, and the elephant heaved its ponderous bulk erect.

"*Salaam*," called Chandra Kumar in farewell, as the beast lumbered away.

"*Salaam*," replied the Pathan leader, and turning, stalked to his tent.

The babu was quite jovial as they rode back toward their own camp, joking first with Kupta, then with Sarkar, the mahout. He was very happy, for though he had forsaken the gods of his forefathers, a new god had taken their place—gold. And he found it very pleasant to contemplate the twenty-five hundred rupees which were the profits of this trip, resting in his heavy money belt along with the money he had mulcted from Kupta and Sarkar. Also, it was exceedingly gratifying to estimate the infinitely greater profits yet to come from this venture.

Within a half mile of the camp, they turned down a side path and halted, it being the babu's purpose to wait there until after the raid had taken place. He and Kupta dismounted and took their ease beneath a shady tree, but Sarkar was content to keep his seat on the elephant's neck while the beast tore off leaves and tender twigs and thrust them into his huge mouth.

Back in the camp of the maharaja, tiffin was followed by the customary nap, which lasted well into the afternoon. Then the maharaja assembled his guests for tea.

For sometime, as was natural, the talk was only of Jan, and the possibility of catching up with him. Naturally, all were anxious to continue on the trail as swiftly as possible, with the exception of the maharaja. But he simulated anxiety on the subject very well.

"There's no use going on," he said, finally, "until we hear from the babu. Also, we must wait for the elephants that are bringing up our baggage. In the meantime," looking at his two male guests, "I think I'll have a try for sambar. There's no fresh meat in camp for my men. And I know of a water hole nearby where the *jeraos*, as we call them, are sometimes thick as fleas. You probably won't care to eat any of the meat—most Americans and Europeans don't, as it is rather coarse in texture. But I think I can promise you two gentlemen some ripping sport if you care to come with me."

Don Francesco turned to Trevor. "What do you say, *amigo*?" he asked.

"I don't know," replied Jan's father. I simply can't get the boy off my mind, and if I thought—"

"Oh, go with him," said Georgia Trevor. "There isn't a thing we can do at present—and you like to hunt."

"Yes, do come," urged the maharaja. "We'll only be gone for an hour or two at the most, and will be back in camp before the babu can possibly get here. Then we'll have a good night's rest and get an early start on the trail in the morning."

"Very well. I'll go. But the ladies— will it be safe to leave them here?"

"I'll leave all my spearmen here," the maharaja promised, "and rifles for the ladies."

We'll take only one elephant and his mahout. Rare sport, shooting from the howdah—and we may flush a tiger."

Shortly thereafter, the maharaja and his two male guests rode away on the back of the largest elephant.

Georgia Trevor and Doña Isabella retired to their couches. Ramona sat down in front of the tent to read a travel book on India which she had in her hand luggage. There was no breeze, the leaves hung motionless on the branches, and the air seemed fairly to quiver with the heat. Several times she caught herself nodding over her book, and presently, overcome by heat-induced drowsiness, she fell asleep in her chair.

When she awoke, the sun had set and a breeze had sprung up. She arose and went for a stroll about the camp. She noticed that wood had been brought in for the cooking fires, but that not one had been lighted. Puzzled, she spoke to an old wrinkled Brahmin beggar who sat a little apart from the others with his back against a tree.

"Why is it you have not lighted your fires and prepared your evening meals?" she asked.

"It is not our custom, *memsahib*," he replied softly. "This interval between sunset and the first glimmer of stars is the moment of silence. No one cooks or lights fires at this time. It is a sacred moment when we sit still, meditate, and listen for the voice of silence."

One by one the stars came out. A man arose and touched a match to his cooking fire.

Then as if this were a prearranged signal, the

silence was broken by the thunder of charging hoofs, and the frenzied yelling of a host of riders, punctuated by the loud reports of rifles and pistols.

Instantly, the camp was thrown into wild confusion. The elephants began milling and trumpeting, their mahouts trying ineffectually to calm them. Then one big bull snapped his tether and fled into the jungle. He was followed by another and another, until all had disappeared into the jungle shadows. The guards seized their spears and ran hither and thither, shouting excitedly.

A dozen black bearded riders charged into the camp, shouting and shooting, their *puggrees* streaming behind them. Others deployed to the right and left.

With frightened cries, the spearmen plunged into the jungle, leaving the camp defenseless.

Cut off from retreat to the tent, Ramona saw Jan's mother and Doña Isabella emerge with rifles in their hands. She saw the former level her rifle at a yelling raider and fire. The raider sprang from his horse and confronted her. Again she fired, point blank at his heart. But he only laughed, wrenched the rifle from her grasp, and pushing both women aside, plunged into the tent. Another rider disarmed the *doña,* and seized her by the arm, while a third, who tried to hold the fiery Georgia Trevor, found he had captured a tartar. She kicked, scratched, and finally seized him by the beard which, much to her surprise, came off in her hands, revealing a scraggy, gray beard beneath it.

The first man then came out of the tent, and spoke rapidly in Pashto.

Ramona, about to rush to the assistance of the others felt a light tug at her sleeve. The old Brahmin who had told her of the voice of the silence was there.

"Come," he said softly. "It is you they want. The others will not be harmed. Follow me. Perhaps I can help you to elude them."

For a moment Ramona stood irresolute. Then she saw the marauders release the two women. One shouted a harsh command, and other raiders began searching the remaining tents. So far none of them had seen her standing there in the shadow. Silently, she turned and followed the old Hindu into the jungle blackness.

THE SNAKE & THE TIGER

CHAPTER VII

A STRANGE FUNERAL

With his right arm and shoulder imprisoned in the crushing folds of the giant python, and the snarling tiger charging straight for him, Jan thought and acted with that celerity which had saved his life so many times before in his native South American jungle. First he leaned far back, then exerting every ounce of his marvelous strength, hurled his burdened arm and shoulder forward. With the backward movement, the coils of the serpent had loosened for a moment, seeking a new grip. Now, the writhing, hissing reptile hurtled through the air, and its heavy coils fell over the head and neck of the charging feline.

Jan caught up the spear and sprang back, but the precaution was needless, for both of his enemies now found themselves so busily engaged with each other that their intended victim was forgotten. The tiger bit, clawed and roared its anger as it rolled over and over trying to rid itself of those crushing folds. But its terrible teeth and talons made little impression on the armored body of the reptile, only dislodging a few superficial scales.

In contrast to the lightning-like movements of the great cat, those of the serpent seemed slow and deliberate. The coils which encircled the tiger's neck tightened into a thick scaly collar. Others slid around its body, the mighty muscles rippling beneath the gleaming skin, constricting, crushing.

Presently, exhausted by its terrific exertions, the tiger ceased its struggles and fell on its side, where it lay breathing heavily.

Watching breathlessly, Jan spoke to the brown boy who stood at his side.

"It kills as kill the boa and the anaconda in my jungle," he said. "The *bagh* is doomed."

"Yes, the *bagh* is doomed," the boy replied, "for the spirit of a Naga dwells in the serpent, and it may not be slain. It is invincible."

"As to that," replied Jan, "I am doubtful. Let us see."

With the spear held in readiness, he warily approached the two combatants. The tiger shuddered convulsively and suddenly ceased to breathe. It was dead, its ribs crushed to splinters; and blood from its fractured windpipe mingled with the foam that drooled from its jaws.

But the serpent was very much alive. As the jungle man drew close, the great spade-shaped head flashed out at him. He eluded it by leaping sideways, then, as it was retracted, sprang in and pinned it to the ground with the long steel blade of the spear. Swiftly the heavy coils of the serpent released the dead tiger. Then it writhed in its death agony while Jan and the brown boy looked on.

"The spirit of the Naga has left it," said Jan. "Its brain is split in two. But it will continue to move for some time. That is the way of serpents."

"It is because the spirit of the Naga has not really left its body," replied the boy. "It may yet slay us."

But Jan only laughed. Then, when the convulsive thrashings of the python began to subside, he seized the tiger by the tail and dragged its limp carcass out of range of the writhing, scaly folds.

"Now we will gather wood," he told the boy, "and cremate your father in accordance with the custom of your ancestors."

The two worked swiftly at their task of building a funeral pyre, and when it was ready, laid the remains of the tiger upon it. Then, after a small fire had been kindled near at hand, the boy walked seven times round the pyre muttering strange words and making queer signs, none of which Jan understood. This done, he thrust a flaming brand from the small fire beneath the heap of wood, which was soon crackling loudly as the flames leaped up around the marauding feline's body, showers of sparks mounting skyward with the smoke.

"What were those strange words you used?" Jan asked.

"I will try to translate for you," the boy replied. "I said: 'O you who are now without a home on the earth, on the rivers or in the sea, depart, and seek not to clothe yourself in flesh again. Go! Go and be with our ancestors! Follow the path of silence where the sun travels, seeking ultimate truth! Go to where the gods await you, for now you must play upon the flute of silence, as death is purified by song.' ''

''A most fitting ceremony,'' said Jan. ''And what will you do with the ashes?''

''I will take them to the Ganges, mix them in a pitcher above the water and say, while I watch the ashes float down the river: 'Travel down with the yellow Ganges into that vast and turbulent entity, the Sea.' ''

The two fed the fire until the tiger was reduced to ashes. These the boy gathered in a large leaf, which he bound with a bit of bark fiber. By this time the movements of python had subsided to nothing but occasional tremors, and Jan recovered the spear.

''It will soon be dark,'' he told the boy. ''Where would you like to go?''

''If we can cross the river,'' the lad replied, ''I should like to return to the camp where there are rice and curry, and from which I can continue on the trail of Rangini, the she-elephant.''

''We can cross the river again,'' Jan assured him, ''so let us start.''

Taking the boy on his back as he had before, Jan managed the leap across the narrow stream in the opposite direction, much to the disgust of the hungry muggers that waited beneath. Before they reached camp the sun had set, and the brief dusk was quickly followed by darkness, the moon having not yet risen.

On their arrival at camp they kindled a fire, and the boy quickly prepared a dish of curried vegetables and rice from the meager stores left by his father. Then disdaining the flimsy, makeshift hut, Jan carried the boy with him into the branches of a tall tree, and there they spent the night.

The following morning Jan, whose jungle appetite was not satisfied by the meager Hindu fare, speared a small hog deer which added delicious grilled venison steaks to their breakfast menu. Having eaten their fill and drunk a satisfying draught from the river, they set out on the trail of Rangini, the she-elephant. After a half day's travel it was evident from the freshness of the tracks that they were getting very close to the great pachyderm. And toward midafternoon they suddenly sighted not one, but two elephants, standing side by side waist deep in the river, enjoying a shower bath, spraying their huge bodies with water sucked up in their trunks. One was a tall female, and the other a tremendous male with long, gleaming tusks.

"It is Rangini!" exclaimed the boy, "and she has come to meet her lover as my father suspected."

"Is this other a wild elephant?" Jan asked.

"No, I recognize him now," the boy replied. "He is Malikshah, the mightiest bull in the herd of the Maharaja of Rissapur."

"Then Malikshah must have broken away also, to meet this she-elephant. Is it not strange that each should know where to meet the other, and when?"

"It may seem strange to one unfamiliar with elephants," the boy replied, "but we who have been born and raised with them do not consider it so."

Fearlessly the boy waded out to the two giant beasts. Then he spoke to Rangini, whereupon she extended her trunk and elevated him to a seat on her broad head. He spoke again, and she lumbered up out of the water, the huge bull keeping pace beside her. Jan, unacquainted with the ways of elephants and ever cautious, kept back out of reach of the two powerful trunks. He closely watched both beasts, endeavoring to determine whether they were friendly or unfriendly toward him, but so far as he was able to tell, both were utterly oblivious to his presence. The boy, however, more experienced and hence keener to observe small indications, said:

"You need not fear Rangini, for she is very gentle, and Malikshah, though he is quick-tempered, seems to like you."

"I do not fear any man or beast," Jan replied. "But these animals are new to me, and caution is the first law of the jungle."

Without further hesitation, he walked up to the giant bull and patted its shoulder; then stood while the great beast sniffed and investigated him with its sinuous trunk. When this investigation was completed, the observant boy said: "Malikshah likes you. I will command him to take you up."

He spoke sharply to the giant bull, and Jan for the first time experienced the strange sensation of being lifted through the air to an elephant's head. He enjoyed it thoroughly, and, once seated on the broad neck, scratched Malikshah behind his great, flopping ears.

"Now that you have your elephant," said Jan, "where do you want to go next?"

"It is my duty to return her at once to my master, the Maharaja of Varuda," replied the boy.

"But what of Malikshah?" asked Jan.

"He should be returned to Rissapur," the boy answered. "Yet it is probable that we will not be able to separate these two at once. They might obey, but would be likely to run away again."

"In that case," Jan replied, "let us take both of

them to Varuda. Then Malikshah can be returned to his owner later.''

''That seems the only thing to do,'' the boy told him after some thought. Then he spoke to Rangini, and the two elephants ambled off through the jungle.

Jan greatly enjoyed the novelty of his ride across grassy plains, over rocky and sparsely tree-grown hills, and through hot, moist valleys luxuriant with jungle vegetation.

Up to this time the boy seemed to have taken Jan rather as a matter of course, but now, with the first part of his duty to his deceased father accomplished, and the elephant with which he had been reared from babyhood safely beneath him, his natural childish curiosity asserted itself.

''O mighty hunter,'' he asked, ''are you of the *sahibs* of England?''

''I am not of the English *sahibs*,'' Jan replied.

''Yet you speak their language, and your hair is colored like that of another *sahib* I once knew— O'Malley Sahib.Though he was a soldier in the English army he swore he was not from England, either, but from the Imraldile. Are you from the Imraldile?''

''I have never heard of it,'' Jan replied.

''Also, he referred to his country as the Owled-sahd.''

Jan shook his head in puzzlement. Then a light dawned upon him. He recalled that one of the sailors on his father's yacht had often spoken longingly of the Emerald Isle and the Auld Sod.

''He must be Irish,'' he said.

''Ah, that is it!'' the boy exclaimed. ''I could not think of the word. And are you Irish?''

"I am an American," Jan replied.

The boy looked disappointed.

I have only seen one American before, a *mem-sahib*," he said. "She had a long, pointed nose and small beady eyes like a crow. I heard that she went back to her country and wrote horrible things about India. Is that what you intend doing?"

"I do not intend to write anything about India," Jan replied. "But if I did it would not be horrible. I like your country very much."

"I am glad," the boy replied, naively, "because I like you very much. Will you tell me your name?"

"My name is Jan Trevor, but I am better known as Jan of the Jungle."

"Of the jungle? Then the jungle is your home?'

"Not this jungle," Jan replied, "but another on the opposite side of the earth."

"Yet you can climb even better than the gibbons and monkeys. Do all men in your jungle climb so well?"

"No, they do not climb nearly so well as even the smallest monkeys. You see I had special training, because I was stolen from my parents when a baby by a very wicked man and raised by a chimpanzee. We both escaped from the man who stole me, but were captured by other men who took us to sea."

"And then what happened?"

"We were shipwrecked on the coast of South America, and escaped into the jungle."

"And didn't you ever see your parents after that?"

"For a few months, I was with them. But now I have lost them again."

"That is sad." A tear trickled down the brown cheek, and Jan sensed that the boy was thinking of his recent bereavement, so he quickly changed the subject.

"You have not told me your name, and how it happens that you speak English," he said.

"My name is Sharma," the boy replied, rubbing away the tear with a small brown fist, "and I learned English in a mission school. Also, my father has worked for many *sahibs*—always he worked for *sahibs* until the maharaja bought Rangini. Then we came with her to Varuda."

Near nightfall they came to a small stream, which the elephants immediately entered. Jan and his small companion left them there and set out in search of food.

Presently Jan succeeded in knocking over a pheasant with a stone, and they soon had it grilling over a fire. When they had eaten, the jungle man constructed a small sleeping platform in a tree. Then leaving the boy with the two elephants, which showed no signs of wanting to leave their bath, he set off on a journey of exploration on his own account.

He had covered not more than a couple of miles when he suddenly emerged into an open, flooded space where a number of men were at work plowing, while women followed them, setting out plants in the shallow, muddy water. At some distance behind them he saw the huts of a small village.

The people were chatting and laughing, and he succeeded in approaching within a few feet of the nearest workers without attracting their attention. What he did not notice was the small, mangy cur which had been ranging in the surrounding jungle.

It suddenly sighted him, and then charged for him, barking loudly.

Though he could easily have slain it, Jan was never a wanton destroyer of life. He killed only for food and in self-defense, and this yapping cur was beneath his notice. But the barking of the dog attracted others, as well as their human masters. A number of men came running, carrying longbladed spears, and the jungle man was soon surrounded by hostile dogs and equally hostile villagers. The latter, who had not yet seen him, evidently thought the dogs had brought some jungle beast to bay and approached warily, their spears held ready for the cast.

Jan let them approach until the circle narrowed to less than a hundred feet. For a moment he was undecided whether to reveal himself and attempt to make friends by means of sign language, or to make good his escape while there was yet time. But the menace of that tightening ring of spears decided him on the latter course.

Suddenly springing from his place of concealment, he clambered up the nearest tree with apelike agility. Instantly a dozen spears flashed round him, but so swift and elusive were his movements that none took effect. The villagers cried out in amazement at sight of this naked white man, who swung off through the interlacing vines and tree trunks with the ease and agility of a gibbon or monkey. They set out in frenzied pursuit of him, but he quickly outdistanced them.

When all sight and sound of the hostile villagers was lost in the distance, he descended once more and made his way back to camp. He called to the boy as he approached the smoking embers of their fire, but received no reply. A moment later he saw to his consternation that both the boy and the two elephants were gone.

The ground was trampled by the tracks of other elephants, many of them, mingled with the tracks of men. Much concerned as to what had happened to his small friend during his absence, Jan made a minute examination of the tracks in order to try to learn just what had taken place.

CHAPTER VIII

THE BLACK PAGODA

Ramona followed the old Brahmin through the jungle blackness more by sound than by sight, though she caught an occasional shadowy glimpse of him each time a break in the forest canopy let in a little light. Presently all sounds of conflict from the camp died away in the distance, and these two were alone in the comparative silence of the jungle—an aged brown man and a young and beautiful girl of the while race. But though the jungle was comparatively quiet, it was far from silent and there were many strange noises which frightened the girl.

The old fellow seemed to sense this and reassured her again and again as they went forward.

"That noise is only made by a tiny insect," he would say, or, "This tremendous clamor is simply a night bird trying to attract the attention of his sweetheart. The really dangerous beasts make little or no noise. If the tiger stalks you, the chances are that you will not hear him until his teeth and talons have pierced your body. Even the mighty elephants can move through the jungle without noise when they wish to do so."

And so they pressed on in this manner until a flicker of yellow light ahead told them that they were approaching a camp.

The cautious Brahmin said, "Wait here. I will go forward to investigate."

"But I am afraid to stay alone in the jungle," the girl replied.

"Why, then come with me and we will both investigate, my child," he replied.

They approached the camp warily and saw that two men were seated beside a small fire smoking cigarettes and chatting. Near the tiny fire was a huge heap of firewood, and lying on the ground nearby were a number of tents packed ready for loading, as well as bales of rugs and other camp equipment. A dozen horses were tethered to the trees not far away.

The old Brahmin squinted thoughtfully at the two men for a moment. Then he said, "They are Pathans—wandering horse traders. We need not fear them. Come!"

He led the way into the circle of fire light.

At this one of the Pathans sprang to his feet, rifle ready, and spoke in Urdu, which of course Ramona did not understand.

"Who are you," he bellowed, "and what are you doing here?"

Then his eye caught the alluring beauty and seductive curves of the girl who stood revealed in the fire light, and his look softened.

"*Bismillah!*" he said to her with a smirk. "Welcome in the name of Allah."

Ramona did not understand a word, but she noticed that his fierce look had suddenly grown friendly, and gratefully accepted the proffered seat on a small rug before the fire.

The Pathan, whose name was Mutiur Rahman, again spoke to the old Hindu. "Are you the servant of this lady?" he asked in Urdu.

"Nay! I am the servant of no mortal who walks the earth," the ancient one replied, "but I have been traveling with the party of his highness, the Maharaja of Varuda."

At this Mutiur Rahman turned to his companion with a slight wink and said:

"Come, Ismail, let us attend to the horses." And, politely to the old Brahmin, "Excuse us for a moment and make yourselves comfortable. We will be with you shortly."

The Pathans walked over among the horses, and as soon as they were out of earshot of the two who sat unsuspectingly beside the fire, Mutiur Rahman said:

"I have a suspicion, Ismail."

"And what is that?" the other asked.

"Is it not strange that these two should be traveling together through the jungle at night, having left the camp of the Maharaja of Varuda?"

"*Subhanullah!*" exclaimed Ismail. "So it is, and the girl—can it be that she is the one our men went forth to capture?"

"Sh! Not so loud or they will hear you," cautioned Mutiur Rahman. "That is exactly what I suspect. Let us return to the fire now and be friendly. But if they attempt to leave we will see that they do not get far."

They returned to the presence of their two unbidden guests, but in accordance with the Muslim custom of not eating or drinking with those to whom they intend possible harm, they made no offer of food or refreshment.

If the old Brahmin noticed this he gave no sign, but sat staring into the fire as if he were looking through and beyond it into another world, his skinny legs crossed beneath him and his wrinkled, bony hands resting upon his knees.

Presently, the rumble of many hoofs caused him to look up apprehensively.

"Were you expecting someone?" he asked Mutiur Rahman.

"Our leader and my comrades rode forth some time ago and should be back by now," the Pathan replied.

The clatter of hoofs swiftly grew louder, and the camp was suddenly clamorous with stamping, neighing horses and loud-voiced men.

Ramona and the old Brahmin sprang to their feet in alarm when they saw that these men, obviously Pathans, ripped off Rajput costumes and huge false beards, which they flung onto the pile of wood nearby.

The Brahmin caught Ramona's hand, whispered, "Come," and attempted to lead her into the darkness. But he was too late, for a huge hawknosed, red-bearded fellow, with a fierce battle-scarred countenance rode up, clove him from crown to chin with a single sword stroke, caught the fleeing girl by the arm, and swung her onto the saddle before him. She kicked, scratched and struggled with all the strength at her command, but found the powerful muscles of her captor unyielding as steel, and only succeeded in making him roar with laughter.

"So! my pretty one, my little white dove," he chuckled. "You saved me the trouble of bringing you to my camp. *Mashallah!* It was well done, indeed, and I thought I had lost you." He turned and roared commands to one of his men who stood beside the pile of wood, clothing and false beards, now reeking strongly of the petrol which had been emptied over it, a blazing brand in his hand.

"Light the fire and we will be off," he cried.

The man flung the faggot to the base of that great pile, which instantly flamed up, lighting the jungle with the brightness of day for many feet in all directions.

The eyes of Zafarulla Khan fell on the body of the aged Brahmin, which still lay bleeding on the ground.

"Fling that carrion into the fire," he ordered. "It is the funeral he would have preferred, anyway, and we don't want to have a corpse here."

As soon as this command had been carried out, the Pathans gathered their tents and equipment, loaded them onto their horses and fell in behind their leader. Then the entire force galloped away into the night.

Presently exhausted by her futile struggles and frightened by the predicament in which she found herself, Ramona went limp and swooned away. Nor did she regain consciousness until the first golden shafts of the morning sun smote her face. Her first glimpse of the rugged countenance of her abductor caused her to scream and renew her struggle. At this he held up his hand and called a halt.

"It seems, my pretty one, that I will be forced to bind and gag you," he said, "as we will soon be on a public highway and you are becoming troublesome."

He bound her wrists together with a silken scarf,

her ankles with another; a handkerchief was forced into her mouth and a second bound over it to keep it in place. Then wrapping a shawl about her so that she was completely disguised and even her face was hidden, he mounted once more, holding her on the saddle before him.

Presently she heard the hoofs of the horses clattering on the paved roadway, and from time to time she heard and caught glimpses through the aperture in the shawl of passing wayfarers. There were carts drawn by bullocks, some empty and some loaded with produce, and all apparently driven by natives of the peasant class. There were automobiles of many varieties, elephants going forth to work in the jungle, haughty, black-bearded Rajputs riding sleek and richly caparisoned horses—a continuous cavalcade, that picturesque hodge-podge of humanity which makes up India.

After a ride of less than an hour on this busy highway, Zafarulla Khan suddenly reined his horse to a halt.

Peering through the folds of the shawl, Ramona saw that they had stopped before a red shrine in which was enthroned a grotesque god, with the head of an elephant and the multiarmed body of a man.

The hawk-nosed leader addressed a few brief orders to his men in Pashto. They clattered off down the road, but he turned aside and rode down a narrow path almost at right angles to it.

Ramona judged that they must have covered about five miles when the Pathan again pulled his horse to a halt. She was uncomfortably warm from the shawl which wrapped her slender body and was therefore relieved when he removed it, as well as the gag.

"You may scream as much as you like now, little dove," he said, "for there is none to hear you except him with whom we keep rendezvous."

She saw that they were on the bank of a broad river and that a man who wore the yellow robe of a priest was propelling a boat toward them.

Zafarulla Khan gave the girl a drink of water from his canteen and permitted her to rest in the shade of a spreading tree on the bank. Then he shouted to the approaching boatman in Urdu, which she did not understand.

"Who are you, yellow robe, and what do you want?" he asked as the boat approached the bank.

"I am Thakoor," was the reply, "and I have come to purchase the white dove."

"*Wallah tayyib*! By Allah, good!" exclaimed the Pathan.

The prow of the boat slid up on the sloping bank, and the priest—an old man whose parchment-like brown skin was a network of wrinkles—stepped out and dragged it higher.

Zafarulla Khan pointed to Ramona.

"There is your white dove," he said.

The old priest scrutinized the girl for a moment in silence.

Then he said. "This must indeed be she, for generations have come and gone since I have seen another as lovely. Here is your gold."

He extended a heavy bag, which Zafarulla Khan hefted suspiciously.

"To what amount," he asked.

"Five thousand rupees," the old one replied. "Will you count them?"

Zafarulla Khan undid the strings of the bag and examined its contents.

"Nay! This seems to be the correct sum," he said, "and I may not linger. But if I find that it is short by a single rupee I will fetch my men and slit the throats of you and all your idol worshipping brethren."

"You will find the sum correct," said the old priest calmly, apparently unimpressed by the threat of the Pathan.

Then he turned his attention to Ramona, untying and unwinding the scarf which imprisoned her ankles.

"Come, my daughter," he said. "You need not fear old Thakoor. He means you well."

He helped her to her feet, leaving her hands bound, but when she flinched and drew back from him, he said, "Come child, be not afraid. Great happiness and undreamed-of honors are in store for you, and I am but the humble instrument of the great gods who order your destiny. Let me help you into the boat."

"If you are friendly why have you left the bonds upon my wrists?" she asked suspiciously.

"An oversight," he hastened to assure her, still propelling her toward the boat. "I will remove them in a moment."

When she was seated in the boat he pushed off and was well out in the stream before he removed the scarf from her wrists. Then he paddled steadily towards the opposite shore.

She looked about her and had a wild notion of diving into the water and swimming away, but the sight of several ugly crocodile snouts caused her to quickly change her mind. For the present there was nothing for her to do except to resign herself to her fate.

As they drew near the opposite bank of the river, several other yellow-robed figures emerged from among the trees and dragged the boat up onto the bank. Again she had the notion of trying to escape, but instantly realized that it was useless, for many of these priests who now stood around her were young and powerful looking men. The old man led her up the bank and through the trees, where a donkey with silvermounted trappings stood patiently, saddled and waiting.

The weary girl mounted and one young priest led the beast away, while old Thakoor walked beside the girl and the others brought up the rear.

The path they followed led first through the trees which lined the river bank, then across a level place covered for the most part with tall jungle grass, and presently once more entered the dense and seemingly impenetrable jungle, in which a walled and roofed path had been hacked with knives. Here moisture dripped from leaves and branches and the brightness of the morning sun was replaced by eerie eternal twilight.

From time to time they broke into open glades where brilliantly colored butterflies flitted about equally brilliant jungle flowers which scented the humid air with their sweet, heavy perfume. And at frequent intervals the girl caught the flash of brilliant bird plumage or saw curious monkey faces peering down at her. There were myriad bird calls, from the twittering of the tiny Java sparrows to the raucous cries of peacocks. And the chattering and scolding of monkeys were audible from time to time.

Presently the path widened and they broke out into the sunlight. Before them was an arched gateway in a high wall of black stone, in which were set two massive bronze gates green and corroded with age.

Old Thakoor shouted something which the girl did not understand and the gates swung open.

When the party passed through Ramona saw that they were in a garden laid out in exquisite taste, with pools, fountains, flowers, shrubbery, and fruit and shade trees. Surrounding the garden, which was laid out in the form of a huge rectangle, were many low buildings, constructed against the high wall which encircled the enclosure. But in the very center of the garden was an edifice which simultaneously aroused both her wonder and disgust. It was built entirely of black stone in the form of a pagoda, which rose skyward, tier upon tier, to a dome supported by square cut, close set pillars. Architecturally it was beautiful, but the creator of this strange building had not stopped with mere architectural adornment, for it was decorated with hideous and disgusting carvings and statues so monstrous that the girl after her first look quickly averted her eyes.

"What is this place? Where are you taking me?" she asked Thakoor.

"You are on holy ground," he replied. "This is the temple of the Mahadevi, the great goddess, Kali, the Black One, and shelters her living reincarnation."

He helped the girl to dismount but did not lead her toward the central building. Instead he conducted her to one of the low buildings against the outer wall of the enclosure. Here a number of girls and women, some chatting and laughing, some quarreling, and all busy with sewing, fancy work and beaded work, looked up at their approach. All conversation ceased on the appearance of the old priest, and he signaled to an ancient and toothless hag, who put down her sewing with apparent reluctance and, rising, came forward.

After she had received brief instructions from the old man, which Ramona did not understand, the old trot took the girl's arm and led her into a building.

Once inside and out of earshot of the priest the old hag cackled toothlessly, "Heh! Heh! Heh! Old Marjanah has been ordered to look after you because she can speak English. Are you hungry?"

"I have not eaten since yesterday," Ramona replied.

"If I were in your place I should not eat anything unless it were deadly poison," mumbled the old hag. "Once I was brought here as you have been brought, and look at me now! It was either this or the teeth and fangs of the Black One."

For a moment fear showed in her eyes and she shuddered as if the very name of the Black One struck terror into her heart. Then she resumed her toothless grin and added, "Come, I will find you something to eat."

CHAPTER IX

PURSUIT

The water hole which the maharaja had said was nearby proved to be a good six miles from the camp. Here a shooting platform had been constructed for some previous hunt, and to this the three men and the gun bearer mounted by means of a ladder, while the mahout took the elephant away.

The hunters waited expectantly at the water hole until sunset without sight of a single sambar.

"Be very quiet now," said the maharaja. "The *jeraos* will soon be coming down to the water to drink."

They waited patiently, but no sambar put in an appearance. The sun dropped below the horizon and the stars blossomed forth in the gathering dusk.

Suddenly Trevor cupped his hand to his ear and said, "I hear shooting. It is in the direction of the camp. Can it be possible that they have been attacked during our absence?"

"I hardly think so," the maharaja replied, "but we will return and find out. No use waiting longer for the sambar. They must have taken fright at something and gone to another water hole.''

He fired his rifle into the air and presently the mahout came up directly beneath their shooting platform with the elephant. One by one they lowered themselves to the beast's broad back and entered the howdah.

''Back to camp! Make haste!'' the maharaja told his mahout.

It was dark when they reached the camp and when they did they found it in the utmost confusion.

Georgia Trevor and Dōna Isabella were frightened and tearful. Only a few of the maharaja's men were in evidence and half of the elephants were gone.

''What is wrong? What has happened?'' Trevor shouted, springing down from the howdah and closely followed by Don Francesco.

''The camp was raided by Rajputs,'' Georgia Trevor replied, ''and Ramona has disappeared. We do not know whether she escaped and has become lost in the jungle or whether the robbers carried her off.''

''Why, this is terrible!'' exclaimed Trevor.

''It is worse than that, *amigo*,'' said Don Francesco, passing a comforting arm about the shoulders of his sobbing wife.

The maharaja had meanwhile dismounted and was now speaking rapidly in Urdu to a small group of his frightened men. After a few moments' conversation with them he returned to his guests.

''I am devastated with grief that this attack should have occurred in my camp and under the eyes of my own men,'' he said. ''Unfortunately, the raiding Rajputs were all armed with rifles, and my guardsmen could do nothing against them with their spears. Also the elephants stampeded and more than half of them have disappeared. The mahouts are out trying to recapture those that have not yet been found. However, I hope that we will be able to take the trail at the first break of day. I know in advance where it will lead because these Rajputs could only have come from Rissapur, and I intend to see to it that they be made to pay for this unwarranted and illegal raid upon my camp in British territory. It must be that they marked the beauty of the girl, and taking her for an Oriental, decided to raid the camp and steal her for their maharaja.

"Do you expect us to wait here all night while Ramona is being carried off by those ruffians?" Trevor demanded.

The maharaja shrugged his shoulders deprecatingly. "Much as I deplore inaction in a case of this kind," he said, "I do not see what else there is for us to do."

"We have flashlights in our baggage," said Trevor. "Give me a gun and, by God, I'll set out on that trail afoot. You may follow at your leisure with your elephants."

"I, too, *amigo*," said Don Francesco.

"Why, if you feel that way about it we will start at once," said the maharaja, coolly adjusting his monocle. "However, as I attempted to explain, there can be but one destination for these miscreants, and that is Rissapur. They have two hours' start on us, and in any event, it will be impossible for us to overtake their swift horses when we have only elephants to ride."

Three elephants were quickly requisitioned. On

the first rode the maharaja and his two male guests, all armed with rifles. The two ladies, similarly armed, rode in the second howdah and behind them came the third elephant bearing a half dozen of the maharaja's guards.

A tracker ran ahead carrying a flashlight. The prints of the horses' hoofs were plain enough in the soft earth and led them directly to an abandoned camp, where the remains of a huge fire smoldered.

"Odd that they should build such a tremendous fire," said Trevor, getting out of the howdah and slipping to the ground. "I wonder why?"

He poked about in the ashes, and at the edges discovered the singed remains of a false beard and several bits of smoldering cloth. These he stamped out and on a sudden impulse thrust all into his pockets for evidence.

Further poking about in the ashes revealed a calcined human thigh bone and several other bones less easily recognizable, but which he judged must be human.

"Some one has been burned—perhaps burned alive here," he cried. "Good God! I wonder—But surely these Rajputs would not have abducted Ramona for the purpose of burning her alive. The Muslims don't do such things, do they?"

"One cannot tell what these Rajputs will do," replied the maharaja. "However, I would not suspect them of that. My men informed me that an old Brahmin disappeared from the camp along with the girl. It is possible that he was slain to seal his lips and his body burned to hide the evidence of the crime."

"Then let us proceed on the trail at once," said Trevor, mounting once more to the howdah.

They rode onward through the night and all the following day. Evening found them on the outskirts of a small village surrounded by rice paddys. The old village headman, accompanied by a number of natives, advanced to greet them.

"Have you seen any horsemen pass this way?" the maharaja asked the old headman.

"Nay, I did not see them, highness, though I heard the clatter of hoofs during the night," replied the headman. "But I saw a much stranger sight."

"What was that?" the maharaja asked.

"Tonight at dusk the dogs began barking near the edge of the paddy fields and my people investigated. They saw a naked white man of marvelous strength and agility, whose hair was the color of burnished copper. They hurled their spears at him, but he escaped by swinging away through the trees more swiftly than a monkey."

"Good Lord! That was Jan! It must have been!" cried Trevor. "Which way did he go?"

"That we do not know," the old headman replied, "nor were we able to find out, as he left no trail, but traveled through the trees."

Trevor shook his head hopelessly.

"I know," he replied. "It was thus he traveled in the South American jungle. If Jan wishes to hide his trail there is no man on earth who can follow him."

He turned to the maharaja.

"Let us proceed on the trail of Ramona," he said. "Perhaps we will again cross the trail of my son."

The half hour's ride brought them out upon a broad moonlit highway.

"As I predicted," said the maharaja, "the trail

leads toward the capital of my neighbor prince. This is the road to Rissapur.''

He had only ridden a short distance along this road when Babu Chandra Kumar came hurrying up behind them, riding his small, swift pad elephant, piloted by Sarkar, the mahout, and accompanied by Kupta, the hillman.

He rode up beside the howdah of the maharaja.

''Where have you been, you fat toad?'' said the maharaja, glaring down at the babu through his monocle.

''Came as fastly as could do, highness,'' Chandra Kumar replied, and continued with a meaning look, ''Is great news abroad among villages. It seems that youngly *sahib*, son of Trevor Sahib is in vicinity.''

''I have already heard that news,'' the maharaja told him, and there was a look in his eyes which caused the babu to cringe. He had told his master that Jan was dead—had believed it himself—and the evidence that he was still alive struck terror into his heart. ''We are following the trail of the miscreants who ran off with the young *memsahib*. In the meantime you will take six men and go in search of the son of Trevor Sahib, and,'' he added meaningly, ''you will bend every effort to find him. Do you understand?''

''Yes, highness, humbly servant understands with perfection,'' said Chandra Kumar.

He nudged the mahout, who kicked the elephant behind the ear, and the great beast turned and lumbered off in the opposite direction.

They had ridden for another mile along the road when they met another party mounted on elephants and just coming onto the highway.

The royal trappings and the magnificent how-dah of the elephant in the lead made it manifest that the beast carried a personage of considerable importance.

The two leading elephants met, and instantly their mahouts caused them to stop and raise their trunks in salute.

Seated in the ornate howdah in solitary state was a large, powerful looking man whose skin was so light that he might have been mistaken for a European. His thick, jet black beard was parted in the middle and combed outward both sides in the manner common among Rajputs. An enormous ruby blazed from the clasp on the front of his white turban and behind it two aigrettes pointed upward. His rich clothing was wholly Oriental, and gems of fabulous value sparkled on his fingers.

As the beasts raised their trunks in salute, he called out:

"*Salaam, maharaja!*"

And the Maharaja of Varuda replied, "*Salaam!*"

Then he introduced his two companions.

"Maharaja, permit me to present Trevor Sahib of North America and Suarez Sahib of South America." And to the two men he said: "This is my friend and neighbor, Abdur Rahman, Maharaja of Rissapur."

The Rajput maharaja acknowledged the introduction with a smile that showed powerful white teeth.

"You honor my little kingdom with your presence," he said. "I trust that I may have the pleasure of entertaining you in my capital."

"We should be delighted, but unfortunately our call is not a social one," replied the Maharaja of

Varuda. "We have come on business of a serious and delicate nature."

"If it is of a private nature perhaps we had best find another place to discuss it."

"No, it is not private, since all within earshot know of it already. Our camp was raided last evening by a band of your Rajput warriors, and a young *memsahib* was stolen. No doubt they made the mistake of believing her an Oriental and perhaps one of your subjects, and will expect your commendation for this act. We demand that the lady be immediately released and that her abductors be punished."

The Maharaja of Rissapur looked dumbfounded.

"Where did this raid take place?" he asked.

"In *British* territory," the other ruler replied with a significant accent on the word "British." "Unless steps are taken to right this wrong at once, I shall be compelled to report the matter to the British Resident."

"Come with me," invited Abdur Rahman. "We were searching for an elephant of mine and found his trail with that of another beast, both evidently stolen by a man and a boy who had built a camp fire nearby. They eluded us, but that matter can wait, in view of this shocking news you bring me. I will make a full investigation at once, and if any of my people have been guilty of such a dastardly act you have my assurance that they will be punished, and that so far as I am able to do so, I will make restitution."

The two parties rode on to Rissapur together, and when he had lodged his guests in his palace, the Maharaja of Rissapur immediately launched an inquiry into the affair of the evening before. But though he set every agency at his command to the task of tracing the miscreants, who were supposed to have ridden straight to the city of Rissapur, he was unable to obtain the slightest trace of them.

At noon, the following day, the British Resident, Sir Cecil Bayne, called.

He was a tall, angular man with a florid face, a tremendous Roman nose and a drooping, sandy mustache.

He was immediately informed of the mission of the visitors, and expressed his regrets that such an outrage should take place in British territory, assuring the distracted friends and foster parents of the girl that the powerful arm of the British Raj would be exerted on their behalf.

The Maharaja of Rissapur continued his inquiries about the culprits who were supposed to be lodged within the city, but in vain. No party of Rajputs such as that described by the two ladies had been seen to enter the city at any time.

After tiffin Sir Cecil sat tête-à-tête with Georgia Trevor on the broad veranda. For the moment the others were out of earshot.

"Really," he said, "I can't understand the Rajputs committing such a crime. I have been the Resident here for ten years and have never heard of anything to equal it."

"Do you know," said Georgia Trevor, "I have been wondering if they really were Rajputs. Our rifles had been tampered with, loaded with blank cartridges, showing that the raid had been planned in advance, and that there was at least one accomplice in the camp, and as I struggled with one of them, I grasped his beard and it came away in my hand.''

"Ah! A planned raid and a false beard,'' exclaimed Sir Cecil. ''A light begins to dawn on me. I shall start some investigations of my own immediately. In the meantime do me the favor of keeping this matter a secret from both of the maharajas. I may have some interesting news shortly.''

''I do hope you will be able to find Ramona soon,'' said Georgia Trevor.

''And I assure you,'' replied Sir Cecil with a bow, ''that your hopes are well founded.''

At this moment the Maharaja of Varuda and the other guests came up.

''I am afraid we can accomplish nothing more here,'' he said, ''and suggest that we start at once to my capital. We should be able to reach it some time this evening if we start immediately. We can then set going the forces at my disposal and operate from there as a base.''

He bowed to the ruler of Rissapur, who had just returned from a conference with his deewan.

''With your leave,'' he said, ''we will take our departure. Your hospitality has been magnificent. I trust that you will pay me the honor of a visit soon.''

''You are most kind,'' Abdur Rahman replied. ''It is my hope that I shall soon be able to bring you news of the *memsahib* and a complete solution of her mysterious disappearance.''

CHAPTER X

THE MAN HUNT

Though he had known Sharma for but a short time, Jan had conceived a strong affection for the little orphaned brown boy, and so when he found that the lad had disappeared from the camp and saw the tracks of many strange elephants and men, he feared that he had met with foul play.

However, careful examination of the river bank showed him that the two elephants, Rangini and Malikshah, had not emerged on this side of the river. Instead he saw the small footprints of the boy spaced wide apart, showing that he had run down to the water to join them. From this he judged that the boy and the two elephants had taken alarm at the approach of the larger party and had crossed the river in order to hide their trail.

Since the stream was so broad at this point that he was unable to spring across by means of the overhanging trees, and the ugly snouts of numerous muggers were in evidence, he decided to build a raft of bamboo. With his sharp jungle knife he quickly

cut a number of large bamboo stalks in the nearest thicket and soon had a raft four feet wide and fifteen feet long bound together with tough, fibrous bark.

With a long bamboo pole in his hand he launched the raft and started across the stream. The crocodiles for the most part paid no attention to him, but there was one, a tremendous fellow, judging by the size and distance apart of the eye and nose bumps which projected above the water, who glided near him and was soon following the raft.

Jan kept an eye on him while he vigorously poled his frail craft toward the opposite bank. But he suddenly learned that it is often inadvisable to try to do two things at once, for the tip of his pole plunged down into the soft mud and stuck there. The raft had meanwhile glided so far ahead that Jan was compelled either to relinquish his hold on the pole or to let the raft glide out from beneath him.

He swiftly decided on the former course, and when he had regained his balance found himself without means of propulsion, as the spear which lay on the raft at his feet was not long enough to reach the bottom in midstream. He tried using the spear blade as a paddle, but made very indifferent progress against the current.

In the meantime the watchful mugger glided closer and closer. Jan could see the dark outline of his body in the water now, and it was tremendous. Frantically he paddled with the ineffectual spear head, and the mugger, as if sensing his panic, suddenly dived beneath the raft. Then its huge tail shot up out of the water and struck the frail craft amidships, shattering the bamboo poles and breaking the bindings that held them together. Jan found himself struggling in the water amid the shattered remains of his raft. Then . a pair of gaping jaws opened to seize him.

He still clutched the spear, so now, treading water, he grasped it with both hands, raised it above his head and rammed it with all his strength down the yawning throat. The jaws clicked shut on the shaft, shearing it asunder, and Jan seized upon the moment of respite to whip out his jungle knife and dive beneath his formidable adversary. He grasped a taloned foreleg with one hand, and hanging on, plunged the keen knife again and again into the leathery belly. The saurian turned over and over in the water, which was now dyed crimson with its own blood, in an effort to dislodge its intended victime who had suddenly become a most dangerous foe. Jan hung on until he knew that his blade had pierced the reptilian heart; then he relinquished his hold and fought his way to the surface.

He saw other menacing snouts converging toward him now, and gripping the knife in his teeth, swam for the bank at his utmost speed. Most of the muggers, however, were deterred by the smell of their comrade's blood and paused where the carcass had sunk to the bottom. Only two kept on after the jungle man, and these he soon outdistanced.

Panting from his exertions, he splashed up through the shallows and onto the bank, where his two pursuers gave up the chase. After a brief rest he set out along the stream in search of the trail left by Rangini and Malikshah, and presently found it about a quarter of a mile below the point where they had entered the water. He drank a deep draft from the river and instantly set out on the trail. It

went straight back into the jungle and was so plainly marked that he could follow it as easily as a
city dweller follows a boulevard.

Presently he began to grow conscious of a gnaw-
ing hunger and kept a sharp lookout for game. The
average white man traveling through this same jungle
would have trod noisily, causing all wild things to
take cover. But the jungle bred Jan instinctively
moved as quietly and cautiously as the beasts themselves. And thus it was that he came suddenly and
unexpectedly into the midst of a group of wild hogs
which were rooting for forage beneath the leaf
mould that carpeted the jungle floor.

The sows and pigs instantly took to their heels
with grunts of alarm, but the old boar, evidently
the patriarch of the herd, stood his ground, lowered
his head and charged. Jan avoided those gouging
tusks by leaping clear over the charging beast, then
before the boar could again face him, turned and
whipped out his jungle knife. The boar instantly
whirled and charged again. Once more the jungle
man sprang over him, but this time he alighted,
facing the rear of the animal. Before the tusker could
turn he had plunged a long knife into its savage
heart.

Jan crouched beside his kill, and was soon din-
ing on raw, warm boar's flesh. He found it exceedingly tough and coarse, but this bothered him not
at all. He had often eaten food that was much
tougher and far less tasty. When he had his fill, he
slashed a rattan, drank the clear water which ran
from the cut end, and, much refreshed, resumed
the trail.

He had expected to be able to overtake the two
elephants in an hour or so, but soon found that

they had traveled much faster than he anticipated
and though he knew he was gaining upon them,
they were still out of sight and hearing when the
sun had reached the zenith.

Shortly thereafter, however, he heard the sound
of heavy animals coming through the jungle and
men talking in a language which he did not understand. He sprang up the nearest tree and out upon
a limb to investigate. Three elephants were coming
toward him, and on the first he made out the con-
trasting forms of the fat Babu Chandra Kumar and
the small, wiry Kupta, both of whom he recognized.
The babu carried a heavy double-barreled express
rifle and a man on each of the other elephants
held a repeating military rifle.

Jan shouted in friendly greeting and the babu
looked up. Then to the surprise and consternation
of the jungle man, he raised the heavy rifle to his
shoulder and fired.

Jan felt a searing pain at his right temple and
crashed downward through the interlacing branches
as consciousness left him.

CHAPTER XI

THE BLACK TIGRESS

The Maharaja of Varuda rode out of Rissapur in the howdah with his two male guests. Shortly after they had passed the city gate they met the maharaja's followers, some on pad elephants and others on foot, bringing up the camp equipment and baggage.

The maharaja ordered them to fall in behind and proceed until they had come to the red shrine of Ganesha, when he ordered a halt and dismounted from the howdah.

"Since we are faced with so difficult a problem," he said, "I am going to make an offering at the shrine of the God of Wisdom and will remain here some time in meditation. My men will conduct you to Varudapur, where I will rejoin you."

He signaled to the mahout of one of the smaller pad elephants and ordered the baggage the beast carried removed and distributed among the others. Then he commanded its mahout to remain and signaled the cavalcade to proceed.

As soon as they were out of sight in the dust of the roadway he mounted the pad elephant and told the mahout to follow the path which turned off from the highway beside the shrine. A ride of several miles took him to the bank of the river at the point where Zafarulla Khan had met Thakoor, the priest, on that same morning.

As soon as the maharaja appeared on the river bank, the two yellow robed figures emerged from the jungle on the other side, tumbled into a boat and swiftly headed across the stream in his direction. As they drew near, the maharaja recognized the wrinkled features of Thakoor in the front of the boat.

"The white dove was brought this morning, highness," said Thakoor as the boat grounded.

"Good!" the maharaja replied, stepping into the boat. Then he called to the mahout.

"Wait here," he said. "I will return shortly after sunset."

On the opposite side of the river a prancing horse was saddled and ready, held by one of the temple guards. Six other guards sat their mounts nearby and immediately fell in behind the maharaja as he galloped off along the trail to the temple. Thakoor also mounted a horse and followed.

When the cavalcade reached the bronze gates of the temple enclosure they were instantly swung wide and attendants sprang forward to seize the maharaja's bridle as he leaped from the saddle.

He waited impatiently until the aged Thakoor came up.

"Where is the white dove?" he asked.

"I have had her installed in the apartment which your highness ordered prepared for her," replied Thakoor, "and have set old Marjanah to watch her."

"I will see her at once," announced the maharaja, starting toward the women's quarters and not deigning to notice the obsequious *salaams* of priests, attendants and laymen all around him.

The guard opened the door of the apartment at his approach, and he entered a tiled hallway where Marjanah, the old hag, sat cross legged on a rug beside the curtained doorway.

"The white dove is within," she croaked, and springing up, drew the curtain aside.

The maharaja strode into the room. At the far end Ramona reclined upon a magnificently upholstered divan, amid soft, silken cushions.

Her khaki clothing had been replaced by a scanty Oriental costume which revealed every seductive curve and line of her slender, youthful figure. Jewels glittered from heavy wristlets and anklets. Her jet black hair was coiffed in the Oriental manner and covered by a web of strung pearls, and her satiny skin exhaled the rarest and costliest of perfumes.

With a start of pleased surprise she sprang to her feet at the sight of the maharaja.

I don't know what magic you employed in order to find me so quickly," she said, "but you are most welcome."

"I must admit that I encountered considerable difficulty in tracing you here," the maharaja replied, smiling ingratiatingly.

"And now you will take me back to my people at once?" she asked. "What of my abductors? Have they been captured?"

"No, but my men are on the trail. As for returning you promptly to your people, there are forces at work with which I am going to find it most difficult to cope."

"But you are the Maharaja of Varuda," she said. "Is not this temple within your territory?"

"That is true," he replied.

"And are you not Varuda's absolute despot?"

"I am the temporal ruler," he answered. "But this is holy ground. In this enclousure the High Priest of Kali is ruler. If I were to attempt to cross him in any way I would have a bloody revolution on my hands and would be sure to be dethroned if not assassinated."

"But surely you can reason with him," said Ramona, frightened at this amazing revelation.

"I have already attempted to do so," the maharaja replied, "but he is adamantine. He claims that he paid five thousand rupees for you this morning and that you have already been consecrated as a sacrifice to the Black Goddess."

"Sacrifice!" she exclaimed in alarm. "What do you mean?"

"Come and I will show," he told her.

He clapped his hands, and the old hag entered the room with a silken shawl which she draped about the shoulders of the girl. Then she held the curtain aside, and as the two walked down the tiled hallway the guard opened the door and *salaamed*.

The maharaja conducted Ramona across the garden and up the stone steps of the Black Temple, where two more guards saluted. Within its portals the air was pungent with the smell of burning incense. But there was another scent, so acrid and powerful that even the sickening sweet incense did not hide it—and though she did not recognize it, it brought to the girl a strange foreboding which she could not shake off.

At first she saw only a gigantic black idol of most hideous aspect.

"It is the image of Kali, the Black One," said the maharaja.

The Black One was a most fearsome sight. Her eyes were red, and her breasts, face and four giant hands were smeared with blood. One gory hand held a sword, one a trident, one a club, but one a shield. Her hair was matted and unkempt, and the tongue which protruded between her projecting fang-like teeth, dripped blood. She wore a necklace of skulls, earrings of dead bodies, and a girdle of serpents, and stood upon the body of Siva.

"Can it be possible," said Ramona, "that human beings actually worship such a hideous object?"

"Some people, yes. They worship the symbol instead of the reality. We enlightened ones worship the great goddess herself and her genuine incarnations."

"You believe, then, that Kali once lived in this horrible form?"

"That is right," the maharaja replied. "She takes and has taken many forms. She is a necessity to earth and to all living creatures, for we require not only to be created and to be preserved for a time —the respective functions of Brahm and Vishnu—but it is equally necessary that we be destroyed again and again in our various reincarnations until we have attained that unutterable bliss and grandeur, incorporation into the body of Brahm. So, like Siva, her husband, Kali carries out the important work of destruction so necessary to all living things in order that they may be advanced toward Nirvana."

"And what would it profit a living creature to lose its identity and to merge as one of the tiny cells with the spiritual body of Brahm?'' Ramona asked.

"Ah! That is a part of our philosophy which you of the West find it difficult to understand or appreciate. The loss of all personal consciousness by absorption into the divine and the extinction of every personal desire and passion leads to the attainment of perfect impersonal beatitude. In that condition we are no longer men; we become gods."

"I am afraid that I could not appreciate a loss of my personality or individual consciousness," said Ramona. "It seems to me that your Nirvana amounts to nothing more than oblivion."

"That is what our early philosophers called it, though they used another term," said the maharaja. "They spoke of it as the 'blowing out.' The human soul, they said, when it attained its last reincarnation was blown out like a candle. Thus all cares and tribulations of the many lives through which we are compelled to pass are lost in the sweet oblivion of oneness with Brahm."

"I can see now why a destroyer is necessary in your system of philosophy," Ramona said. "You spoke of sacrifice. I believe you said that I have been brought here as a sacrifice to Kali."

"That is true," the maharaja replied. "Since Kali is a destroyer she loves blood—wallows in it— drinks it." He pointed to the black idol which towered above them. "Look at the blood on her hands, smeared upon her breasts and on her face! See the gore that drips from her tongue! Every life snuffed out through a human agency is a sacrifice to her, which will bring manifold blessings upon the one who makes the sacrifice. And the great goddess is especially pleased at the sacrifice of handsome young men and beautiful women.''

''Then I was brought here to be slain to appease this monstrosity?'' Ramona asked.

''To please the great Black Mother,'' the maharaja corrected. ''She has been especially gracious to her devotees in this temple as she has appeared to them in living form.''

''You mean in the form of a woman?''

''No, I will show you.''

He led her closer to the pedestal on which the giant idol stood, and she noticed for the first time that it consisted of a cage, the sides and front of which were iron bars.

There was a barred door in front of the cage, and at the rear a door of bronze was set in the black stone wall: It was from this cage that the powerful and acrid scent which Ramona had noticed on entering the temple emanated—the scent of a great cat and of partly decayed flesh. On the floor of the cage lay part of a gnawed spine, a slender brown finger tipped with henna and a fragment of a human skull to which the black hair still clung.

Closely watching the effect of his words on the girl—for he had a definite plan in telling and showing her all this—the maharaja smiled as he noted the horror in her eyes. Now for the climax!

He drew back a lever at the side of the cage. The bronze door in the rear swung open. For a moment a pair of slanting eyes gleamed redly in the darkness behind it. Then a great black cat sprang out into the cage. Not a leopard, but a huge tigress whose glossy fur was black as jet—one of the rarest color phases of this animal.

Ramona involuntarily drew back with a gasp

of dismay as the tigress upon sighting her emitted a roar and sprang furiously at the bars through which the girl peered. The maharaja flung a supporting arm around her as she seemed about to faint.

"Come," he said. "I did not mean to frighten you, but you were curious to learn the fate which had been prepared for you and I thought it best to show you."

He led her out into the sunlight once more, where she conquered the vertigo which had assailed her. But she could not shake off the feeling of horror which the sights in that black temple had engendered.

Having returned her to her apartment, he said, "I must go now, though you may rest assured that I will do all in my power to save you. However, the decision as to whether you will be saved or not rests with you."

"How is that?" Ramona asked.

"If I were to claim you as my bride, my *maharanee*, and furnish a slave girl to take your place, the priests would be compelled to consent to the exchange."

Ramona looked at him searchingly for a moment.

"A light begins to dawn on me," she said. "I have observed how every one in this temple, even the high priest himself, regards you as his lord and master. It is you who had me kidnaped and brought here—you who staged this horrible display in order to frighten me into marrying you. I tell you now once and for all that rather than marry you or any other man living except Jan Trevor, whom I love, I would voluntarily walk into the cage with that black tigress which you pretend to believe is a reincarnation of your ugly blood-thirsty goddess.''

The maharaja bowed calmly. ''I see you have determined to misunderstand me,'' he said, ''and at the moment I have no time to argue the point with you. Suffice it to say that the truth will make itself manifest in good time. Your sacrifice has been set for some days hence, so you will have ample time to reconsider if you care to do so. If not, just as sure as there is a sun in heaven, Kali will claim you for her own, and neither I nor any power on earth can save you.''

Screwing his monocle into his eye, he again bowed formally, and turning, strode out of the room.

CHAPTER XII

MALIKSHAH TO THE RESCUE

The babu uttered a cry of exultation when he saw Jan crashing down through the branches.

"Good shot! Very excellent shot!" he chuckled. "Let me down so I may make sure of him."

He prodded Sarkar, the mahout, who caused the elephant to kneel, and ran toward his victim accompanied by the blood-thirsty Kupta, who already had his *kukrie* in his hand, and by several spearmen.

But there was another who had heard Jan's shout and the shot which followed it. Malikshah, the bull elephant, had been feeding by himself in a little glade not two hundred feet away.

He pricked up his ears, raised his trunk and sniffed the breeze. No, his ears had not deceived him, for he recognized the unmistakable scent of the *sahib* whom he had instinctively liked at first sight.

He climbed up out of the ravine with a rapidity remarkable in a beast so huge and trotted toward the spot where his trunk told him the jungle man lay. And scarcely had he arrived within sight of the fallen Jan when he saw a group of brown men coming from the opposite direction. Some carried guns, some spears and one a huge wicked looking knife. And the wise, old Malikshah instinctively knew that they meant no good to his friend who lay helpless and bleeding on the ground.

Trumpeting angrily, he charged the approaching group with stiffened trunk and tail. The babu took one look at the charging bull, cast his heavy gun upon the ground and turned to flee. The others, equally frightened, dashed off into the underbrush on both sides, leaving their leader to his fate. It was soon upon him, for he was a most indifferent runner. The sinuous trunk wound about Chandra Kumar's fat waist. Then he was swung aloft and hurled through the air to alight among the branches of a scrubby pandanus. Although the tree saved his life, it did so most painfully, as the saw-edged leaves pierced his tender flesh in a thousand places.

Malikshah trumpeted belligerently and looked about for the others, but all had disappeared; so he returned to where Jan lay.

Tenderly he nuzzled the jungle man with his trunk, but elicited no response. Finding it impossible to arouse him, he picked up the limp body and strode away, making for the spot where he knew Rangini would be feeding, attended by Sharma.

Presently he found them in a sun-dappled glade. Rangini was contentedly stuffing tender leaves and twigs into her huge mouth, with the little brown boy lazily stretched out at full length upon her broad back, inhaling the fragrance of an orchid which he had plucked from its lofty perch, and watching the birds, bees, and butterflies that flitted around him.

At first he paid no attention as Malikshah came toward them, but when the huge bull drew closer he instantly recognized the limp burden dangling from his trunk.

He spoke sharply to Rangini, who lowered him to the ground, then ran toward Malikshah and patted his trunk. Gently the giant beast laid the unconscious man on the ground.

Sharma uttered a cry of consternation when he saw that his friend's face was covered with blood, which had drained from a long furrow in his right temple. They were a considerable distance from any water, so the lad searched until he had found a suitable rattan. Then he made a cup from a folded leaf and filled it with the cold, clear and slightly bitter sap. With this he returned to the side of Jan, whose fluttering eyelids foreshadowed returning consciousness.

Raising the blood-smeared head, he held his improvised cup to the jungle man's lips. Jan sputtered, choked and then swallowed the liquid, which seemed to revive him. He opened his eyes and looked up into the brown ones of Sharma.

"Where are we? What happened?" he asked.

"I don't know," Sharma replied. "Malikshah brought you here just now and some time ago I heard the report of a rifle in the distance. I believe you have been shot."

"That is true. I remember now," Jan replied. "It was the babu who shot me. I called to him, believing him my friend, yet he raised his gun and fired."

"Perhaps he did not recognize you," said Sharma.

"Perhaps," Jan answered, "but that is doubtful. He knew me well enough, and I have not yet solved the mystery of the attack on me which took place on board my father's yacht. He may have been the one who tried to kill me before, and having failed, tried again."

But why should this babu wish to kill you? asked the boy. "I have seen him for many months in the service of the maharaja, and he always seemed a gentle, jovial soul. His one great weakness was his love of money."

"That may be the solution," said Jan after some thought. "Perhaps someone has paid him to kill me. It will bear investigation."

Though dizzy from loss of blood, Jan rose to his feet. His wound throbbed painfully, but had bled sufficiently to cleanse itself, and was closing.

Jan signaled to Malikshah, who lifted him to a seat on his head.

"Which way is the river from here?" he asked.

"I will show you," Sharma replied.

Resuming his seat on the neck of Rangini, he spoke to her and she started off through the jungle, with Malikshah lumbering behind her. Presently they came to the river, where Jan washed the blood from his face and drank deeply.

"I have lost my spear," he said, "and it seems that we have need of other weapons, not only for hunting but for protection. If you will look around for some small, sharp bits of stone for arrowheads I will see what I can do toward making bows and arrows."

The jungle man searched for an hour before he found wood tough enough for his purpose. But once he had found it, he swiftly hewed out two bows with the keen jungle knife—a large and powerful one for himself and a smaller one for the boy.

Twisted bark fiber made stout, tough bow strings, and reeds provided light, straight shafts for the arrows.

When he returned to the river bank he found that Sharma had collected quite a heap of small jagged stones. From among these Jan selected a number, which roughly simulated the shape of arrowheads, patiently chipped and notched them and bound them to the shafts he had brought with him.

"Now we will require feathers to make the shafts fly true," he said. "I saw some pheasants a while ago, and they will not only supply the feathers but the meat of which we are in need. Wait here and practice with your new bow and arrows."

Sharma stuck a branch into the sand for target and practiced assiduously for more than an hour. At the end of that time Jan returned with a brace of pheasants. While the jungle man plucked and skinned the birds, Sharma gathered wood and lighted a fire. The two dined on grilled pheasant and had for dessert a mangosteen, an evil smelling but delicious tasting fruit, which fell from a tall tree nearby before they had finished their meat course.

Their meal over, the two set to work to feather all the arrows they had manufactured, and the versatile Sharma wove two quivers from rattan while Jan scraped and polished the rough cut bows.

They had completed their labors and were assembling material with which to build a sleeping platform in a tall tree nearby when Jan suddenly caught the scent of strange elephants and men. So keenly developed from his years of jungle life was his sense of smell that he could not only distinguish the scent of men, but could discern between individuals. And so he knew without seeing him that the fat babu was following.

Malikshah and Rangini were having their afternoon bath in the river at a point about a quarter of a mile from where Jan and Sharma stood, so they had not sensed the approach of intruders.

"Wait here," Jan told the boy. "The babu and his men are following us and I am going to see what they are about."

Grasping a thick vine, he went up hand over hand and swung off through the interlaced branches. Soon he came within sight and sound of the party that had followed him. The babu had regained his rifle and was riding upon the leading pad elephant as before.

But Kupta preceded them on foot, his eyes glued to the trail.

As Jan looked down upon them from his concealment of his lofty perch, Kupta turned and spoke rapidly in Urdu. Though he could not understand the words, Jan knew from his gestures that he was telling the babu they would soon be upon their quarry.

There was no doubt in Jan's mind now that the fat Chandra Kumar was bent on killing him.

So he nocked an arrow, drew it back to his ear, took careful aim at the fat figure of the babu and released it. The twang of his bow was followed by a choking cry from Chandra Kumar as the arrow pierced his fat neck. He clutched at it for a moment, then swayed and would have fallen had it not been for the mahout, who turned when he heard his cry, and caught him just in time to prevent his fall. At the first twang of the bow, Kupta scuttled behind the elephant.

Jan fitted a second arrow to the bow string, and this time took aim at the rifleman who sat on the second elephant. Again the heavy bow twanged and the arrow buried itself to the feathers in the man's breast. He pitched from his seat without a sound. There were cries of alarm from the others, and the entire party turned to flee. But before they could get out of bow shot, Jan managed to bring down the last rifleman.

Jan watched them go, a grim smile upon his lips.

So frightened were they at the deadly accuracy of their unseen enemy that they did not pause to recover the bodies of their comrades or the guns.

As soon as they were out of sight, Jan descended and examined the two men he had shot. Both were dead. He stripped off their bandoleers, took their rifles and left them where they had fallen.

Returning to the river bank where Sharma waited, he said, ''The enemy has retreated. I don't think they will return to bother us again today.''

Instead of sleeping at that spot as they had planned, Jan and Sharma walked into the shallows and waded down to the river to where the two elephants were enjoying their bath. Then they mounted and rode off into the jungle, continuing until nightfall, when they found a tall tree which provided them with a safe dormitory.

In the morning Sharma aroused Jan at the first peep of day and proudly exhibited two mouse deer which he had slain with his arrows.

''Some day,'' he said, ''I shall be a mighty hunter like you.''

"You are already a skilful hunter," said Jan, "as these little animals are very elusive. Since I have come into this jungle I have not been able to kill one of them. How did you do it?"

"I arose very early while the stars still blossomed in the garden of the sky," replied Sharma, "and built a small blind. Then I used a device to attract the deer which my father once showed me. They call to each other by beating on the leaves with their feet.

"I closely imitated the sound by beating upon a leaf with two sticks. Presently a deer came and I missed him because of the poor light, but when the second and third came I shot them."

The two descended from the tree, and after a breakfast of broiled venison set out on the trail of the two elephants which had wandered away during the night. They found them feeding in the jungle about a mile away, and mounting, rode off.

Jan wished to put as much distance as possible between them and the scene of the previous day's encounter, as he thought it quite probable that the men who sought to kill him would be likely to return with reinforcements and again take up the trail.

They rode on through the jungle until the late afternoon, when Jan, who was swiftly learning how to manage Malikshah, suddenly brought the beast to a halt and sniffed the air with quivering nostrils.

Sharma also stopped Rangini and asked, "What is wrong? Has the enemy come up with us again?"

"No," Jan replied. "This is a new scent, though one very familiar and very dear to me. Ramona is somewhere nearby." Slowly he guided the great beast forward until they came to a high wall of black stone.

By springing up from the back of the elephant, Jan was able to catch the edge of the wall and draw himself up. He saw an immense garden, in the center of which stood an ornate building of black stone, decorated with hideous carved statues in hideous postures.

Yellow-robed shaven-headed priests wandered about in the garden, and here and there groups of women and girls laughed and chatted.

He looked about for Ramona, his heart hungry for a sight of her. Up until the time the babu had taken a shot at him he had suspected her of attempting to kill him that night on the yacht.

Now he was extremely doubtful, though he could not be sure that the babu was not in her pay. The latter had been lent to his father by the maharaja for the purpose of serving them and showing the party about Calcutta, and of course the jungle man knew nothing about the fate of the yachting party following the attempt upon his own life and his miraculous escape into the jungle.

For some time he crouched there on the wall, straining his eyes for a sight of the girl he loved, but in vain. He knew she was here, somewhere—knew that scent too well to be mistaken.

Crouching low in order that he might not be observed, he crept across the tiled roof in the direction from which the scent came. He was near the edge of the sloping roof when a loose tile slipped out from beneath him. Wildly he clutched at another, but this one also came off in his hand and he slid over the edge of the roof. It was a twenty-foot drop, but Jan had fallen head foremost, and despite his agility, was unable to turn himself in the air in time to prevent injury.

He struck on his left shoulder. His head collided with the flagstone paving, and oblivion claimed him.

CHAPTER XIII

THE BABU'S STORY

By urging his elephant, which was the swiftest beast in his herd, the maharaja hoped to catch up with his guests before they reached Varudapur. But he had not covered more than half the distance when he overtook the three elephants he had sent out to hunt Jan, traveling in the same direction.

He noticed with some surprise that his two riflemen were missing and that the babu, who rode on the foremost elephant, was solicitously supported by Kupta, a blood-soaked cloth wrapped around his thick neck.

"Now what, fat swine," he said, glaring at the babu as he came up to him. "Have you fallen off your elephant? And where are your other two men?"

"This babu is very sickly man, highness," said Chandra Kumar. "Most dangerously wounded. Had encounter with redhead jungle *sahib*. Both slain with stone-tipped arrows like that which came near ending this reincarnation for humbly servant."

"You mean to say that this man with a primitive bow and arrow defeated three of you who carried rifles?" said the maharaja.

"Once I shot him down from tree top," said the babu, "and we would have finished him then and there, but an unfriendly bull elephant charged, scattering men and hurling humbly servant into shrubbery."

"As soon as you return to Varudapur," said the maharaja, "you will get in touch with my guardsmen, and while I do not wish to make the offer official, you may tell them that a reward of five thousand rupees will be paid for the head of this savage jungle man. The head must be brought secretly to you and you will be empowered to pay the reward.

"When you catch up with the others you will say that you saw the young *sahib* and attempted to signal him, but that he evidently took you for an enemy, wounded you and killed two of your men, and so you were forced to retreat. Understand?"

"Understanding is perfectly, highness," the babu replied.

They overtook the rest of the party at the city gates of Varudapur. The maharaja then resumed his seat on the howdah with his two male guests and they continued to the palace—an imposing structure of marble and carnelian, age weathered and representing the Hindu architecture of five centuries before.

The Trevors' party was given luxurious suites, and the maharaja excused himself because of much state business which had accumulated during his absence.

As soon as this was attended to he went straight to Mr. Whitaker, the British Resident of Varuda. Whitaker was a wizened, bespectacled, sun-dried specimen of humanity who had spent the greater part of his sixty years in India.

"I trust that you have enjoyed your vacation, *maharaja sahib*," said the British Resident, waving his caller to a seat.

"Unfortunately, *sahib*, it has been marred by a most unpleasant incident," the maharaja replied, "two of them in fact."

"Not really," drawled Whitaker. "Sorry to hear it. Anything I can do about it?"

"There is much you can do about it," said the maharaja, "and it should be done soon. But I will begin at the beginning: I met a party of interesting Americans in Singapore and we became very friendly. They were on their way to Calcutta, so I lent them Babu Chandra Kumar to act as their guide and interpreter because of his familiarity with Calcutta and environs.

"Then I returned here and left to do some deep sea fishing, using the permit you so kindly obtained for me so that I might legally cross and hunt in British territory.

"Some days later I sighted the yacht of my American friends, apparently in distress, and on investigation found that the son of the owner had leaped or fallen overboard. Next day we saw his tracks leading into the jungle, so knew that he had reached the shore alive, and set out to find him.

"He is a most extraordinary youth and I understand lived the life of a savage in the South American jungle up to a few months ago. We found that he had frightened a number of villagers, and later he slew two of my men who were searching for him, apparently taking them for enemies, and wounded the babu himself.''

''Quite a dangerous fellow, I take it,'' said Whitaker. ''It seems that he must be treated as a wild man. Perhaps he can be captured with nets or something of the sort, what?''

''I believe it would be safest to have his parents and friends head the search parties for him,'' the maharaja replied. ''Surely, he won't try to kill them? But I have not told you the worst part of my story.''

''Eh! How is that?''

''When we were encamped for the night in British territory I left the camp with my two male guests to have a try at bagging some sambar. While we were gone the camp was raided by Rajputs, and the Suarez girl was kidnaped. We trailed her abductors straight to Rissapur.

''On the way we met Abdur Rahman, but the Muslim maharaja disclaimed all knowledge of the affair and pretended to make inquiries. Of course, the inquiries came to nothing. So we left him warning him that if the girl were not returned there would be serious consequences.''

''This is indeed a most grave matter,'' said Mr. Whitaker. ''I shall communicate with my superiors at once.''

''In my opinion,'' said the maharaja, toying with his monocle, ''this Rajput who has forsaken the religion of his forefathers is a most dangerous person and a menace to the peace and security of India. He should be removed.''

''He shall be,'' Mr. Whitaker promised, ''if investigation proves that he is back of this dastardly plot.''

The maharaja screwed his monocle in place.

''I must return to my guests now,'' he said, ''so we can organize search parties for both of these young Americans who have disappeared. There is little hope of finding the girl, however, unless we search the seraglio of Abdur Rahman, which will of course mean war.''

''I think he will submit to the British Raj without a war,'' said Mr. Whitaker, rising. ''To do otherwise would be plain suicide. I will get busy on this matter at once and you will hear from me shortly.''

On his return to the palace the maharaja found his guests driven almost to distraction by worry and inactivity.

''Have you learned anything?'' Georgia Trevor asked him as he entered.

''Nothing as yet, I am sorry to report,'' he said, ''but I have not been idle. I have just reported the entire affair to Mr. Whitaker, the local British Resident, and he has promised me the aid and support of his government. I am sure this Rajput upstart will be compelled to release Miss Suarez in the next day or two. In the meantime we can organize searching parties for the boy, but before we do this, I wish to call in the babu who has some information for you.''

He clapped his hands, and a servant appeared in the doorway.

''Send in Babu Chandra Kumar.''

A few moments later the portly babu waddled into the room. His fat neck was swathed in clean white bandages and his face had an unwonted pallor.

"You will tell the *sahibs* of your experience this morning," said the maharaja.

"Was heading search party for youngly *sahib*," said the babu, "looking in the vicinity of village where he was last seen. Then saw him perched on limb of tree. Shouted to him to come down with friendly gestures, but he shot stone-tipped arrow which pierced my neck. This babu fainted away from pain and loss of blood, but when conscious once more, found that two of men had been slain by young *sahib*, and he had disappeared."

Trevor, who had been pacing the floor nervously, stopped and faced the babu.

"Do you mean to tell me that my boy made an unprovoked attack on you and your men, wounding you and killing two of them?"

"Very sorry to have to make such report," the babu answered, "but have very painful evidence here on neck."

"Do you think the terrors and privations through which he has passed have driven him mad?" asked Georgia Trevor, looking up at her tall, sun-bronzed husband.

"Nothing of the sort," Trevor replied. "There is something fishy about this. Some of these men must have appeared hostile or Jan would not have attacked them."

The babu shook his head sadly.

"Were very friendly," he said, "but perhaps youngly *sahib* did not recognize us and took us for enemies."

Trevor glanced at the portly figure of the babu. "If he failed to recognize you," he said, "he needs to have his eyes tested. But what are we to do now? That is the point."

"I was coming to that," the maharaja said. "I intend to organize three large search parties and suggest that you, Trevor Sahib, head one, Suarez Sahib head another and I head the third. The babu is too badly wounded for the rigors of jungle travel and judging from his first experience his second encounter with the young *sahib* might prove fatal. However, I am sure that unless, as Mrs. Trevor has suggested, he has been driven mad, he will not be hostile toward any of us.

"Does this plan meet with your approval?"

"Yes."

He turned to Don Francesco.

"And you, *sahib*?"

"I think it is a splendid idea," the Don replied.

"Then I will see that preparations are made, and we will start in the morning, allotting different territory to each search party," the maharaja replied. "Now let us go in to tiffin."

CHAPTER XIV

LITTLE EARTHQUAKE

When Jan came to his senses after his fall to the flagstones in the temple enclosure he thought at first he was dreaming. For it seemed to him that the sights and sensations which greeted his returning consciousness could not be real.

He was lying stretched out on a cushioned divan, and his head was pillowed on the silk-clad thigh of a slender brown-skinned dancing girl, who bent over him, bathing the aching bump on his head with cold water. He attempted to sit up, but she restrained him and spoke softly in a language which he did not understand.

He replied in English: "Who are you? Where am I?"

She answered in the same language but with a strange accent that was not unpleasing.

"Lie still, *tuan*! You had a bad fall beside the doorstep, and my attendants helped me to bring you here. Fortunately, the priests and guards did not see you."

"But who are you?" he asked.

"I am Jamila, who dances in the temple of Kali, but I am better known as Gempa Ketchil, which means 'Little Earthquake' in my native Malay language."

"Then you are not a Hindu?"

"No, I am Malayan. The dancing girls are selected not because of race but because of ability. There are three Kashmiri girls, several from Tibet, one from Egypt and two from Japan, as well as the native girls. But all have been taught the temple dances and ceremonies of Kali."

Despite her protestations, Jan sat up and looked around the gaudily furnished room. There were taborets containing mirrors, cosmetic boxes, trinkets, and other odds and ends. Upon one a small pot of incense smoldered, filling the room with the mingled scent of musk, sandalwood, ambergris, and jasmin.

"And now that I have told you who I am," said the girl, "perhaps you will tell me your name."

"I am Jan Trevor," he replied, but I am better known as Jan of the Jungle."

"You are English?"

"No, American."

"You are the first American I have seen," the girl told him. "I did not know that the dress of the Americans was so different from that of the English."

"It isn't," Jan replied. "I don't dress like other Americans since the jungle is my home. I am very thirsty. Can you tell me where I can get a drink of water?"

"I have been most thoughtless," the girl replied. "You shall have both food and drink immediately." She clapped her hands and a slave girl entered.

"Bring food and tea for my lord," she said.

The girl withdrew, and presently returned with a tray containing several vessels, from which emanated the savory odors of curry, steamed rice and Darjeeling tea.

Jan ate until his hunger was satisfied.

Then the girl said, "You have not told me how you happen to be here. Did you drop from the sky?"

"No, from the roof," he answered. "I was looking for a girl."

"You have come to the right place, my lord," she replied, "but it is very dangerous. If the priests or guards find you, you will be fed to the Black One."

She moved over and snuggled against him.

"You were very brave to come here, *tuan*," she said. She took his hand and drew it around her slender waist. "And I love you for it," she concluded.

Jan withdrew his hand. "But I came here in search of a girl I know," he told her.

"What is the matter with me, my lord?" she asked. "Is this other more beautiful than I?"

She stood up and piroutted before him, displaying the seductive lines of her lissom figure.

"Surely you could look further and fare worse, as the English say. I will dance for you, and you will never wish to leave me."

She went to the doorway and called another girl, who came in carrying a small drum. The girl seated herself and began a throbbing cadence on the instrument, while she softly hummed a plaintive melody in a minor key.

Jamila instantly began her dance, the like of

which Jan had never seen before. A dance which spoke of love and longing and desire in a language which anyone might understand.

Before the dance had reached its conclusion, Jan understood why the girl was called "Little Earthquake."

Her dance over, she flung herself at his feet, panting and exhausted, looking up at him with amorous eyes.

"Take me in your arms, jungle man. Love me. Jamila is yours," she said. But Jan pushed her away.

"I have tried to make it clear to you," he said, "that I came here for another girl—the one girl I love."

Jamila sprang to her feet, eyes blazing.

"So Jamila is not good enough for you," she shrilled.

Suddenly she snatched a knife from a nearby taboret and sprang at him like a tigress. As the knife descended towards his breast, Jan caught her wrist and wrenched the weapon from her, then held her as she attempted to bite, kick and scratch him.

"Let me go!" she screamed. "You fool! You brute! I will call the priests and the guards. You shall pay for this insult to Jamila."

Thakoor, who was passing the dancing girls' quarters at the moment heard her infuriated screams. He ran into the building, peered through the curtains and then shouted for the guard.

Jan saw him, sensed the enmity in his look, and releasing the dancer, looked about for some avenue of escape. The door in which the old priest stood was the only means of egress, so he bowled Thakoor over and plunged out into the temple enclosure, then looked for a way out.

The guards, armed with rifles, were running toward him from all directions. At sight of him they brought their weapons to their shoulders, shouting to him in a language which he did not understand. But he realized that they were calling upon him to halt and that to attempt flight would be suicidal.

Old Thakoor, who had not been badly injured, appeared in the doorway and shouted a command to the guards, two of whom sprang forward and seized Jan's arms. The jungle man flung them off, and instantly there was a scrimmage, with Jan as its focal point, and a half dozen guards beating, gouging, kicking and pulling at him. One after another Jan flung them from him, but each time he rid himself of one of the tenacious guards, it seemed that two more took his place. Presently exhausted by his herculean efforts, he was borne to the flagstones and bound hand and foot.

When they had him helpless the aged priest issued a sharp command. Four men lifted the jungle man and bore him across the garden into a side door of the black temple and down a winding stairway which seemed to lead into the very bowels of the earth. Here he was flung into a tiny cell, dimly lighted by a faint yellow radiance which filtered through a tiny aperture from overhead.

As he lay on the floor panting from his exertions, bound and helpless, old Thakoor said:

"So! You would pollute this sacred ground with your presence and profane a dancing girl with your touch. For this you shall be sacrificed to the Black Mother."

Then he turned and left the cell, the barred door clanging behind him.

Jan was left alone in the darkness. For some time he struggled ineffectually with his bonds. Presently exhausted, he fell asleep. When he awoke his ears told him that he was not alone, as something slithered across the floor in his direction. He caught the acrid scent of a serpent, and drawing himself to a sitting posture, saw an enormous hooded reptile, with head upreared coming toward him. It was an immense king cobra, the most fearsome and deadly of all serpents.

Again Jan made a superhuman effort to burst his bonds, but the tough fibers held, and he knew that nothing short of a miracle could save him from death.

CHAPTER XV

THE HARVEST OF GOLD

Promptly at sunrise, the morning after their arrival in Varudapur, Trevor and Don Francesco in cork helmets, khaki and shorts, met the maharaja in the courtyard of his palace. The latter was a picture of sartorial splendor with his immaculate turban, eyeglass, and white tropicals, and was smoking his inevitable cigarette.

"The gods have favored us with a beautiful morning, gentlemen," he said. "I trust that they will smile on us as we make our search today."

"Let us hope so," Trevor replied, fishing out his pipe and tobacco. "They have frowned continually, lately. Shall we be off?"

"Always restless, always impatient, you Americans," said the majaraja. "But in this case, you have a most excellent reason. Yes, let's be off. I have divided my eighteen available elephants among the three of us. So we will each have six, as well as a party of spearmen on foot. You, Trevor Sahib, will search the territory which lies toward the northwest, and I will search toward the northeast. The best plan will be for each party to spread out in as wide a line as possible, the leader's elephant at the center of the line, and the others spaced at regular intervals on either side, with spearmen

145

in between. By following this plan, we should be able to comb Varuda from one end to the other in a couple of weeks, or less.''

''An excellent plan,'' said Trevor. ''Which is my elephant?''

The maharaja raised his hand, and one of three elephants equipped with ornate howdahs and standing at the other end of the courtyard, came forward. The beast raised its trunk in salute, and the attendant lowered the ladder.

Trevor mounted, and the maharaja called up to him.

''Your party awaits you at the northwest gate,'' he said.

Suarez mounted the second elephant, and the maharaja the third. Georgia Trevor and Dõna Isabella, who had been watching from the balcony, waved farewells and wished them success, as they rode away.

The maharaja had been very careful to see that neither of his guests should ride in the direction of the Black Pagoda. Also, the territory which he had assigned to himself was that which not only included the blasphemous Temple of Kali, but the one in which he thought it most likely that he might find Jan. The men who rode on his elephants were secretly armed with rifles, and he carried several himself, ostensibly for big game. But their real purpose was to make sure that the jungle man should not again escape.

As soon as his forces had spread out in a skirmish line, the hidden rifles were brought out. They hunted until mid-afternoon without a trace of the man they sought. Then the maharaja called a halt for rest and refreshment, at his pleasant summer place in the hills, midway between Varudapur and the Black Pagoda.

They had taken but a brief rest, when a temple guard arrived. The maharaja was strolling about the camp, smoking a cigarette, while his men lolled in the shade. Among these men was Kupta, the hillman. The latter pricked up his ears as the temple guard approached the maharaja and waited leave to speak.

"Well, what is it?" snapped the maharaja.

"Thakoor sends great news, highness," the guard replied. "The young *sahib* of the flaming hair has been captured."

"Where is he now?" asked the maharaja.

"Confined in a cell beneath the House of the Black Mother," the man replied. "He cannot escape."

"He shall not escape," the maharaja rasped. "I'll see to that, personally. We leave for the temple at once."

He turned to Kupta.

"You are a good runner, hillman," he said. "Go back to my palace and tell the *memsahibs* I go to the Black Pagoda to beseech the Mahadevi, the Great Goddess, for the safety of the young *sahib* and *memsahib*. Your ears have heard nothing else—your eyes have seen nothing else. If they betray me, you will part with them at our next meeting. Do you understand?"

"Yes, highness," replied Kupta.

"Then be off!"

Kupta caught up his spear and sprinted away.

Babu Chandra Kumar, whose activities had been curtailed by his wound, was reclining at his ease in his quarters, chewing his quid of betel and discoloring the rim of his brass cuspidor, when Kupta slunk in as silently as a shadow and squatted on the floor.

"Back from the hunt so soon?" the babu asked.

"I bore a message from his highness to the *memsahibs*," the hillman answered.

"What was the message?"

Kupta repeated it.

"Hum," reflected the babu. "So he has gone to the Black Temple. Did a messenger come from the temple first?"

"That I am not permitted to say," the hillman replied.

"So! There was a message from Thakoor!" He adopted a wheedling tone. "Come, my friend. We have no secrets from each other. You and I are comrades—bosom friends. What was the message?"

"I am not permitted to tell either what I have heard or seen," was Kupta's dogged reply.

"Well, there are other ways," smiled Chandra Kumar, blandly. "Come here."

Kupta advanced and helped himself to a quid of betel which the babu proffered. Then he seated himself beside the brass cuspidor.

"You cannot be punished for anything *I* think, can you?" asked Chandra Kumar.

"That is true," replied Kupta, mumbling contentedly.

"Now assuming that you are me, and you know there has been a message, what would you guess that it contained?" asked the babu.

"News of great importance," replied the hillman. "Any fool would know that."

"Right," agreed Chandra Kumar. "And the news of the greatest importance to his highness at the moment would be the killing or capture of the young red-headed *sahib*, let us say, by temple guards. If you were me, which would you assume were the case?"

"I may not answer," said Kupta, doggedly.

"Well, then, we'll put it in still another way, in which there will be no harm in answering," wheedled the babu. "Which would you assume was not the case?"

"That he had been killed," replied the simple Kupta.

"Ah! So the maharaja is hurrying to the temple to see that he will be killed!" For some time the babu considered the situation, and what possible profit there might be in it for himself. He had been absent from his home in Howrah for several months and was very anxious to return. Furthermore, he was not deceived by the maharaja's promise that he might make him his *deewan*, as he knew the potentate held him in considerable contempt.

While this bothered him not at all, for he was accustomed to being held in contempt by pompous princes and nabobs, it obliterated any slight sense of loyalty which he might have toward his employer. So he decided it was high time for him to collect whatever money might still be obtained from this venture and leave for Howrah. Accordingly, in the late afternoon he rode forth on his donkey, accompanied by the faithful Kupta in the direction from which he expected Harry Trevor to return. Knowing the man to be a millionaire, he felt sure he would pay a huge sum for the information which the babu had to offer.

Presently he saw the string of elephants coming along the road, and hailed Trevor as he came up.

"*Salaam, sahib!*"

"*Salaam*, Chandra Kumar," Trevor replied. "What brings you here in such a hurry?"

"Have very importantly news for Trevor Sahib alone," Chandra Kumar answered. "Will *sahib* condescend to dismount and speak with this less than insignificant person in private?"

Trevor signaled his mahout. The ladder was lowered from the howdah and the American descended. The babu led him off to a side of the road.

"Humbly servant is very poor man, *sahib*, with extremely large and hungry family in Howrah," said the babu. "Would Trevor Sahib be willing to pay this very inferior person for information as to whereabouts of the *memsahib*, as well as his son?"

Trevor looked at him suspiciously. "Do you mean to tell me that you know where both of them are?" he asked.

"Know for positively honest-to-golly where both can be found," the babu answered, "and for lakh of rupees will divulge information. Cannot do so for less as tremendous personal risk is involved. This babu takes life in hands to even whisper of such matters at all."

"From whom would you be in danger?" Trevor asked. "The Rajputs?"

"No, *sahib*, that I will not say or any more until the money is produced."

"Why, I haven't so much money with me," Trevor told him, "but I can give you a check."

"Check will do," the babu answered. "Make it out and will divulge information. If not correct and as humbly servant has said, *sahib* can have this babu arrested for swindling.''

Trevor hesitated for a moment. He did not trust this wily Bengali and yet after all, what was a lakh of rupees or a thousand for that matter, compared to the safety of his son and Ramona Suarez? He got out his checkbook and fountain pen.

''Make out check to cash, please,'' said Chandra Kumar, but at this Trevor demurred. ''The check must be made out to you and endorsed by you,'' he specified, ''since I will have no other receipt or guarantee of your integrity.''

''Very well, *sahib*. To me, then,'' he answered.

Trevor wrote the check for a hundred thousand rupees and held it until the ink dried while the babu looked on.

''Well,'' he said, ''the information.''

''*Memsahib* was abducted by order of the maharaja himself,'' the babu said, ''and was taken to the temple of Kali, hidden in the jungles to the northwest of Varudapur.

''A man named Thakoor is the nominal high priest of the temple, but the real high priest is the maharaja himself, and it is said that he makes many bloody sacrifices there each year. Am not worshipper of Black One and never attended ceremonies, so that part is only hearsay to me. However, believe that the maharaja intends marrying the *memsahib*, and know positively that he will order the young *sahib* sacrificed to Kali.

''If you would save them, go to Mr. Whitaker, the British Resident, organize rescue party and start at once.''

Trevor was dumbfounded, and yet the more he thought of the various phases of the case, the more he was convinced the babu was telling the truth. It was clear to him now that the maharaja had lured the two white men away from the camp in order that it might be left unguarded for the raid. It explained also the fact that the guns left for the women had been loaded with blank cartridges, and that the supposed Rajputs were not Rajputs at all, but others in disguise.

He also had heard the rumor of the impending amalgamation of Varuda and Rissapur and knew that one of the two monarchs would have to be deposed, so it did not take him long to determine the motives back of all the maharaja's actions.

He suddenly extended the check to the babu, and turning, hurried to his elephant.

"Back to Varudapur quickly!" he told the mahout as the ladder was drawn up. "This is a mission of life and death!"

He stopped at the residence of Mr. Whitaker, and fortunately found him in, the latter having just completed his afternoon siesta.

Swiftly he explained the situation to the Englishman.

"Really, this is most extraordinary," said Mr. Whitaker, "most extraordinary, indeed. In fact, I am inclined to doubt the whole story. However, since the safety of your son and the daughter of Don Francesco is involved, I will do my best to make an investigation.

"I have a guard of twenty Sepoys who will be ready to leave in half an hour. We'd better use horses in order to save time. I will lend you one of mine, and will also have a mount for Don Francesco if he returns in time."

As soon as the babu received the check from

Harry Trevor, he rode for Varudapur as fast as the donkey could carry him and made for the stall of one Ishaak el Yahudi, a Hebrew money changer of his acquaintance, who did quite a flourishing business in Varudapur.

After a violent argument with the Jew, which lasted nearly an hour, the babu suceeded in cashing his check for what he insisted was a ruinous discount of ten percent. This transaction concluded, he rode to his own quarters, packed his suitcase, and remounting his donkey, made straight for Rissapur.

He reached the capital of Abdur Rahman's little kingdom in the evening, and immediately sought audience with the maharaja.

The latter, who was entertaining guests, at first said that he would not recieve him until tomorrow, but the Bengali sent back word that his news was very urgent, had to do with the *memsahib* who had presumably been kidnaped by Rajputs, and could not wait.

Upon learning this, Abdur Rahman said, "Conduct the babu to the reception room. I will see him there."

The Rajput maharaja made excuses to his guests and said he would be gone but a few minutes, then entered the reception room, where he found the babu waiting.

The latter was hot, tired and dusty from his long, grueling trip, and quite pale from the illness induced by his wound.

He waited for the ruler to address him, as was customary.

"*Salaam, babuji,*" said the maharaja. "If you have an important communication get it over with quickly, as I have left my guests in order to receive you.''

''This babu stands before your highness, a wounded, ill and impoverished man,'' said Chandra Kumar, ''all because of working for the Maharaja of Varudapur in a clerkly capacity, but not remaining in his employ because of his nefarious plots.''

''Eh! What's that? Plots did you say?'' asked the maharaja, pricking up his ears.

''Humbly servant will be glad to reveal all to your highness for a small sum of money to defray the expenses of return to Howrah, where large and hungry family awaits him,'' he said.

''What do you mean, a small sum of money?''

The babu considered for a moment. He knew that Abdur Rahman was not especially wealthy, as maharajas go, and was afraid he would defeat his purpose by asking too large a sum, as he could not expect to get as tremendous an amount of money as the fabulously wealthy American had paid him.

''For ten thousand rupees will reveal all, highness,'' he said.

''The sum is ridiculous,'' Abdur Rahman replied, ''and how do I know that your information will not be worthless?''

''It is information that will preserve your highness' kingdom for you,'' the babu answered.

''Why, then, if you are the custodian of such information I can call the guard,'' said the Rajput ruler. ''There are other ways of obtaining information from you besides paying you for it.''

The babu cringed. ''Nay, do not call the guard. Am very sick man and must get on train for Howrah at once in order that may have nursing of family.''

''I will give you five thousand rupees,'' the

maharaja said, ''provided your information is what you claim it to be. You have my word of honor on that, so speak now and do not detain me longer.''

''The raid on the camp of the maharaja of Varuda was planned by himself,'' the babu said, ''and the raiders were not Rajputs but Pathans in the pay of his highness, disguised as Rajputs.''

''Ha! I suspected as much,'' said the maharaja. ''Who was the leader of these villainous Pathans?''

''None other than the notorious Zafarulla Khan,'' the babu replied.

''And what was done with the girl?'' the Rajput wanted to know.

''She was taken to the Black Temple of Kali.''

''What of the red-headed jungle boy?''

''He followed her there and was taken prisoner. He is to be sacrificed to Kali, and the young *memsahib* forced into marriage with his highness.''

Abdur Rahman clapped his fist upon his palm.

''*Wallahi*! I see it all now,'' he said, ''and I am convinced that you speak the truth.''

He clapped his hands and a servant appeared in the doorway.

''Tell my treasurer to fetch five thousand rupees at once,'' he said. ''Order my horse saddled and tell my guardsmen to divide into two parties, one of which I will lead myself. The other party, under the lead of Mahmood, will immediately start out in search of that Pathan villain, Zafarulla Khan.''

The babu waited only long enough to receive his money from Abdur Rahman's treasurer. Then he hurriedly took his departure for the railway station, which was a mile and a half from the city of Rissapur.

CHAPTER XVI

FED TO THE TIGRESS

When he saw the cobra coming toward him in his dark cell, its hooded head swaying and its tongue darting menacingly, Jan strained at his bonds until he was bathed in perspiration, exerting all the strength of his powerful young muscles.

Presently a strand snapped, then another and another, and his hands were free. By this time the serpent was almost upon him. There was no opportunity for him to unbind his ankles, but he rose to his feet and sprang back just as the serpent struck, avoiding death by a mere fraction of a second.

There ensued a race around the tiny cell, which apparently could have only one outcome, Jan hopping backward with his ankles bound together, while the serpent followed, striking again and again at his unprotected legs.

Presently Jan thought of a plan which might give him some respite. Suddenly crouching he leaped for the narrow barred opening in the ceiling.

He caught hold of an iron bar and drew his legs up out of reach of the enraged snake. But the bar was old and rusty, and illy supported by the ancient mortar in which it was embedded. The strain was too much for it and one end tore out of the groove.

At this Jan caught hold of another bar which seemed to be stronger. The first had come out in his hand. Now he was no longer defenseless, but armed with a weapon which would at least give him equal chances with the serpent. The cobra was coiled directly beneath him, its hooded head raised threateningly.

Jan thrust the bar into his belt, and untied the bonds which prisoned his ankles. He swung his body back, then forward in a long leap which carried him into the far corner of the cell. Instantly he turned to face the cobra, which promptly started toward him.

When the snake was nearly within striking distance, Jan lashed out with the bar. The reptile dodged the blow and struck back, but with cat-like quickness, the jungle man eluded it and brought down the bar on the reptile's head. It writhed on the floor for a time while he beat that venomous head into a mass of bloody pulp.

Then as he flung the still squirming reptile into a corner, he heard the sound of approaching footsteps on the stairway outside. A guard bearing a torch in his hand had heard the commotion and was coming to investigate.

Quickly Jan resumed his recumbent position on the floor, laid the rope over his ankles and held his hands behind him.

The guard unlocked the barred door and entered the cell. He spoke rapidly in a language which Jan did not understand and the latter made no reply, so he came and bent over him to see if his bonds were in place.

Instantly Jan tripped him, and before he could rise, brought the heavy bar down upon his turbaned skull. He went limp without a sound, and the jungle man knew that he was unconscious for some time, if not dead.

Jan realized that it would be impossible for him to get across the temple enclosure without a disguise, and although this guardsmen was slightly smaller, he believed he would be able to get into his uniform.

It did not take him long to possess himself of the man's clothing, turban and weapons. He also helped himself to his jailer's keys, and took the precaution of locking him in the cell before leaving.

Since the sole light which came to him was from the flickering cressets within the Black Temple, and since he had slept for an unknown time, he did not know whether it was day or night. So after he had mounted the stairway, he was relieved to find that the sun had set, and therefore felt confident that his disguise would be effective, as his face was sunburned to the brownness of a light colored Hindu.

Imitating the self-important swagger of the temple guard, he walked through the garden toward a tall tree, the spreading branches of which overhung the roof of the low buildings constructed against the wall of the temple enclosure. If he could reach that tree undetected, he felt sure that he could make good his escape, after which he would find some way to return for Ramona.

But it was his misfortune to blunder directly into the path of the little wizened, lynx-eyed Thakoor. The priest, who knew every temple guard, instantly saw that this youth, whose long arms and legs and swelling chest were very poorly covered by the clothing he had purloined, was the prisoner intended for sacrifice to Kali.

"Ho, the guards," he shouted, "the jungle man is escaping!"

He leaped in front of Jan, who thrust him out of the way and ran for the tree which had been his objective.

In the dim twilight his flying figure was not an easy mark to hit, and though rifles were popping and bullets whistling all around him, he managed to reach the tree unscathed.

He scrambled up into its protecting branches, dropped to the tiled roof of the building and ran across it to the edge of the wall, from which he sprang into the jungle.

When the Maharaja of Varuda arrived at the Black Pagoda he was met at the gate by Thakoor.

"Where have you confined this wild jungle man?" he asked Thakoor, the priest.

"Alas, highness, he has escaped," Thakoor replied.

"What! How did that happen?"

"It appears that a cobra got into his cell and so frightened him that he broke his bonds. He is as strong as ten ordinary men, you know. Having broken his bonds, he wrenched out an iron bar, slew the cobra and brained a guard who went to investigate. He took the guard's clothing and was crossing the enclosure when I saw and recognized him. I shouted, and the guards fired at him, but with no apparent effect, for he climbed a tree, went over the wall, and escaped into the jungle.

"Fool! You had things in the hollow of your hand. Now you have bungled them. You should have slain him at once. Now we don't know what to expect. Well, there is only one thing to do. I must either marry this girl at once, or let her be devoured, so that no trace will remain of her when the *sahibs* come. For they will surely come, now. And if they find her here an unwilling guest, my kingdom is doomed, this temple is doomed, and you and I are dead men.''

''To feed her to the Black One at once would be the wisest plan, highness,'' said Thakoor.

''We will let her decide that point,'' said the maharaja, ''but she will have to decide quickly. Where is she?''

''In the apartment your highness has set aside for her. She is being prepared for the ceremony—for *either* ceremony.''

''I'll go and have a talk with her.''

The maharaja found Ramona being prepared for the ceremony in which she was to be an unwilling participant. Slave girls anointed her with sweet smelling unguents, stained her fingers and toes with henna, and draped her with jewels.

When she looked up to see the maharaja standing in the door, she noticed that he was no longer attired in semi-European costume and that he had dispensed with his monocle. Now he wore the ceremonial robes of a High Priest of Kali.

The slave girls hung the last string of jewels in place and departed noiselessly. Then the maharaja spoke.

''I have come for your decision,'' said he.

''I have already told you what it would be,'' Ramona replied.

''You must think this over carefully,'' he urged, ''for it rests entirely with you whether you will live to be a wealthy and pampered *maharanee*, or whether that fair body will be torn to pieces and devoured by the Black One.''

Ramona rose and fixed him with a cold glance.

"You may rest assured of one thing," she said, "and that is I will never marry you."

At this the iron calm of the maharaja suddenly broke. To Ramona's astonishment he flung himself on his knees before her—abased himself.

"Ramona," he said, "if you have no pity on yourself, then have pity on me. There are a thousand beautiful women I might have for the taking, but it is only you I want—only you I love. I have been married before, yes, many times. What man in my position has not? But until I looked into your eyes I never knew the meaning of true love. I never knew the tortures and heartaches, yearning and loneliness that separation from one's beloved brings. If I cannot have you, then life will not be worth the living."

"And you would feed me to a tigress!"

"I shall feed you to the Black One, yes. But ere another week is past I shall sacrifice my own body to the same Black Mother. Oh, Ramona! Have pity on me! Can you not find it in your heart to love me just a little?"

"I can find pity, yes," she replied,. "and a considerable measure of loathing. But no love. You speak of love, but do not know the meaning of the word. To you it is mere sensuality. To me, love is spiritual. It is unselfish. It seeks to protect its beloved rather than to destroy. You say you love me, yet because I do not willingly come to your arms, you threaten me with a horrible death. Do your worst, maharaja of thousands, but base slave of your own passions! I defy you!"

Slowly he rose to his feet. It seemed that his face had aged ten years in as many minutes. His usually square shoulders had a despondent droop as he turned wordlessly, and departed beneath the brocaded curtain which the slave girl obsequiously held back for him.

He crossed the temple enclosure without looking to the right or left, walked up the steps, and entered the central room where the blood-smeared multi-armed black monstrosity looked down at him. Seating himself cross-legged in an attitude of meditation, he remained there in long silent suplication to the Black Mother.

All his life, the maharaja had been pampered. When he was a child his parents pampered him. And as soon as he was elevated to the throne, his subjects had pampered him. Very soon after his accession to the throne, numerous subjects with lovely young daughers had presented them to him for his *zenana*, hoping to curry favor with their young sovereign. Neighboring potentates had sent him beautiful dancing girls. Presently as he grew older, he had set himself up as a connoisseur of beautiful women. That was his sensual side. But he had also a religious side. By inheritance and tradition, he was a devotee of Kali, as his ancestors for untold generations had been before him. A remote progenitor had built the Black Pagoda, which to this day was maintained by a considerable sum set aside from the revenues of Varuda. His ancestors and many of their subjects had been Dacoits, Thugs, to whom the commission of all forms of crime, and especially murder, was a religious obligation. Thuggee had been abolished by the British, but the criminal caste remained, and practiced many orgies in secret of which the British Raj never dreamed.

However, he had had an Occidental as well as

an Oriental education. He was an Oxford graduate. And the facts and philosophies he had learned in England had also become a part of his being. He had learned the English ideas of love and chivalry —and it was the conflict between these two opposite codes which was now taking place in his soul.

He had spoken the truth when he told Ramona she was the first girl he had ever loved. Previous to his meeting with her, women and girls had been mere toys, to be played with and dismissed. But genuine love had come to him unbidden—really unwanted. And since he had had no legitimate way of appeasing it, he had taken the Dacoit's way—the way of his criminal caste—to force Ramona's capitulation. Had she been of the Orient, this method might have proved successful, as it might have even with many Occidental girls of a certain type.

Now, with Jan at large, with almost certain exposure facing him, he realized the enormity of the crime he had committed, and the price he would undoubtedly be compelled to pay. Only Ramona's willing assent to marriage with him could save him. He had failed in securing that, and now there was but one alternative. She must disappear from the face of the earth, in order that no trace of his crime would remain. To accomplish this end, the means was at hand—the black tigress. And for him to employ any other means after going this far, would be to lose caste with his blood-thirsty followers and fellow worshippers.

He went through a hell of torment as he sat there, contemplating the ugly, blood-smeared face of his black goddess, whose features seemed at times to actually move in the orange light from the flickering cressets, and whose red eyes stared down at him unpityingly through the drifting haze that rose from the smouldering incense.

Presently he was aroused from his unpleasant meditations by shouts, and the sound of shooting. He rose and went to the door.

"What has happened?" he asked the nearest priest.

"A band of Sepoys led by *sahibs* is attempting to force the gate," replied the priest.

The maharaja shouted for his captain.

"Ho, Rajam," he called. "To me." The captain came running.

"Who is at the gate?" asked the maharaja.

"Whitaker Sahib with his Sepoys, and two other *sahibs*," replied Rajam. "Thakoor refused to let them in, and they began shooting. I ordered my men to return the fire, and they retreated into the jungle."

"Keep them out at all costs," ordered the maharaja.

As the captain hurried away to carry out his instructions, he entered the temple once more and signaled to a priest, who struck a tremendous gong a single resounding blow.

"It is time for the sacrifice to begin," said the maharaja. "Form the procession and bring the white dove."

Once more he resumed his seat and his attitude of meditation.

Presently there appeared a long procession of priests, dancing girls and musicians. The latter, seating themselves at one side of the room, played a barbarous melody, and the dancing girls, led by "Little Earthquake," went through the temple dances of sacrifice to Kali.

During this time Ramona was held by two priests before the door of the cage, which was still empty, but she heard snarls and thunderous growls issuing from the enclosure beyond, and knew that the black tigress was thirsting for her blood.

At this moment there came the sound of a fusillade of shots from outside the temple. Thakoor slipped up beside the maharaja and whispered in his ear.

"They have returned to the attack," he said. "Shall we go on with the ceremony?"

"Our guardsmen can hold them off until the end," said the maharaja. "We will continue."

The musicians struck up another plaintive minor air, and the priests joined their voices in a chant that pealed upward and reverberated from the temple dome.

Louder and louder grew the chant, and louder and louder played the musicians, while thunderous blows on the huge temple gong added to the tumult.

The maharaja took a last, lingering look at the lovely regal little figure before the cage. "What a *maharanee* she would have made for me!" he thought. But he did not speak. Instead, he raised his hand.

At his signal, two dancing girls stripped the jewelry from Ramona. An attendant opened the door of the cage, and she was thrust inside.

As the door clanged shut behind her the one in the rear of the cage swung open. Two glowing red eyes peered out.

"Farewell, beloved," groaned the maharaja.

Then the black tigress sprang for her victim.

CHAPTER XVII

A BATTLE OF GIANTS

Jan's first act, after he had made his escape from the Black Temple, was to rid himself of the cumbrous clothing of the guardsmen, which impeded the free motion of his limbs.

Since his own weapons had been taken from him, he retained the heavy, keen bladed sword which, he noted with satisfaction, had been honed to an almost razor-like sharpness by its owner. After he had belted the weapon to his waist, he began to look for his friend Sharma, the little brown boy, and the two elephants, feeling sure that they were not far off.

Although the moon had not yet risen and it was too dark to see the trail, he soon found it by scent, and followed as swiftly and easily as if the huge pugs of the elephants had been plainly visible to him.

Presently the waning moon came up, making the trail visible in all but the deeper recesses of the jungle. Then he heard Malikshah trumpet.

A moment later, he came out in an open glade near the bank of the river. The place was evidently a ford, for the bank was flattened on both sides by the tracks of numerous beasts and vehicles, and a road wound away from it in both directions.

He caught sight of Sharma, at once. His little brown friend was seated on the neck of Rangini. A little way from them stood Malikshah. The big bull's trunk was raised belligerently, and his huge tusks gleamed white in the moonlight. It was obvious that something had angered him—but what?

Jan gazed into the jungle shadows at the far side of the glade. Something was moving there— something huge and bulky. It trotted out into the moonlight, a giant tusker as big as Malikshah. Its attitude, too, was belligerent. For a moment it stood there in the open, sniffing the air speculatively with upraised trunk—then trumpeting angrily, it charged.

With equal celerity, Malikshah sprang forward. The two met midway with a terrific collision that shook the ground. Then they began savagely butting and gouging each other until the shoulders of both were slashed and gored in many places.

Jan ran across the glade to where Sharma sat on the neck of Rangini. The boy, intent on the battle of the giants, did not see him until he called.

"Ho, Sharma. Where does the strange elephant come from?"

"He is a pariah," the boy replied, "an outcast from all elephant herds because of his wicked temper. I have heard of him, but this is the first time I have ever seen him. He has killed three bull elephants, and many men, women, and children. Hunters have been looking for him, but he has

always been too cunning for them. Men call him
Yama, the Evil One, the King of Hell. But his time has
come. Malikshah, the mighty fighter, will kill him.''

Indeed, for a time, it did seem that Malikshah
was getting the better of his fierce adversary, as
they fought back and fourth across that trampled
arena. Swiftly he forced the pariah back along the
river bank, and away from the ford.

Suddenly the pariah felt soft mud behind him—a
sink hole. He knew that another step backward
would doom him to defeat and death. But he was
a cunning brute—had it not been for this he would
not have lived so long to kill helpless natives and
terrorize whole villages. So he pretended to give
ground, then suddenly flung himself to one side.

Malikshah plunged forward, intending to wheel
and renew the attack. But he discovered, too late,
that he was in soft, yielding mud. He floundered
desperately in an effort to save himself, but his
struggles only sank him more deeply into the soft,
clinging mire. Soon his legs were completely imbedded
and still he was sinking.

Yama stood watching him for a moment, speculatively. Then, knowing his powerful adversary to
be helpless, sprang forward to finish him. Malikshah trumpeted his anguish as the keen tusks pierced
his side.

As soon as Malikshah begun sinking into the
mire, Jan sensed the precarious position of the
beast who had saved his life. He sprang forward.

''Come back, *sahib*!'' cried Sharma. ''You can
do nothing! The pariah will kill you!''

But Jan only ran forward the faster, whipping
the keen sword from its sheath. He came up behind
Yama just as the pariah was beginning the thrust

which was to end the earthly career of Malikshah.
Then he swung the sword in a terrific blow that
half severed the left hind leg of the pariah.

Yama whirled about, trumpeting in anguish,
his little mad eyes glaring their hatred. Then he
charged, which was precisely what Jan wanted him
to do. Swiftly as a deer, the jungle man bounded
away, leading the limping killer from his helpless
victim. Having crossed the glade, Jan plunged into
the jungle and swung himself up into the trees. The
mad elephant crashed in after him, following more
by scent than sight, his questing trunk sniffing and
exploring.

Presently he located the jungle man in the tree
above him. Instantly, he applied his broad head
to its trunk, and pushed.

Feeling his perch toppling beneath him, Jan
sprang into another tree. In a moment the first had
crashed to earth. Seeing that he was not upon it
the mad elephant turned, and soon located him
again by scent. Once more he applied his head to
the tree in which the jungle man sat.

Jan might easily have escaped by swinging off
through the branches, but he did not want to leave
the crazed killer here to wreak his fury on the helpless Malikshah, and perhaps on Rangini and Sharma as well. So instead of trying to run away, he
carried the battle to his enemy. Drawing his sword,
he dropped onto the broad back.

Instantly the beast's trunk whipped up to seize
him, but Jan was ready for that. His sword flashed,
and four feet of the trunk flew off and fell writhing
to the ground.

At this, Yama snorted in helpless rage and pain,
and once more dashed out into the open glade.

Since he could do nothing to the hateful being on his back, he charged straight for the first living creatures that met his gaze—Rangini and Sharma.

Jan thrust his sword to the hilt in that broad back, in the hope of finding the huge elephant heart, but with no apparent effect. Then he withdrew it, and moving forward thrust it into the giant neck beside the cervical vertebrae. He sliced toward the giant spinal column until the blade caught in a crevice between the vertebrae—and kept on slicing.

Yama charged up to where Rangini stood. She avoided his charge, and turning, inserted her trunk beneath one of his tusks and over another. She held him thus, for a moment, then gave a tremendous heave, intending to throw him off his feet. But by this time, the sword of the jungle man had sliced half through the brute's cervical vertebrae. The sudden heave of Rangini completed what the sword had started, snapping the monster's spine asunder with a sharp cracking report.

For a moment the dread killer swayed on his feet, his bloody head twisted grotesquely to one side. Then he sank to the ground, dead.

Jan sprang to the ground.

"Come," he said. "We must get Malikshah out of the mud, or he will sink so deeply there will be no help for him."

Sharma urged Rangini after the jungle man as he ran to where the giant bull was mired.

They went to work methodically—the man, the boy and the two elephants.

First Jan and Rangini brought large sticks and logs which they placed in front of Malikshah. The big bull helped them, pulling the material up close to him with his trunk. Then Jan wove a stout rope from jungle creepers, with a large knot at each end. Malikshah grasped one knot between his huge molars and wound his trunk around the rope. Rangini took hold of the other end in a similar manner, and pulled.

But Malikshah was a heavy elephant, badly mired, and it looked for a time as if even the tremendous strength of Rangini would be of no avail. Finally he succeeded in getting a foreleg out of the clinging mud, and up onto the logs which had been placed in front of him. More tugging on the part of Rangini, and up came another foreleg. In a moment he was free, and on solid ground once more.

Trumpeting joyously, he went first to the carcass of his fallen foe, sniffed it for a moment, and then ambled down into the water, where Jan scrubbed him thoroughly with a large flat stone.

When he had rid his mount of the clinging mud, Jan had himself lifted to the huge head and rode out to the river bank, where Sharma and Rangini waited.

At this moment, he heard the clatter of horses' hoofs coming from across the river. Turning, he beheld a party of horsemen approaching. Instantly suspicious that they were enemies, he called softly to Sharma, and the two rode into the shadows.

The horsemen splashed across the ford. Jan saw that there were more than a score of them. They paused at sight of the huge bulk of the slain elephant. One of the riders, a little wizened white man, dismounted.

"Now what could have slain that beast?" he asked in English. "Good lord! Not only is he badly gored, but part of his trunk is missing! And his neck is broken and partly severed!"

One of the native riders spoke up.

"I know not how he met his fate, *sahib* but he has come to a most fitting end, for this is Yama, the pariah, the killer, the most feared elephant in all India. Only last week he slew my little brother and sister in a raid on our village."

Then another voice spoke up.

"Come, Mr. Whitaker. We have more important business than this post-mortem over a rogue elephant. Let us ride on."

At sound of this voice, Jan suddenly urged his elephant out into the open.

"Father!" he shouted, sliding to the ground.

Harry Trevor instantly flung himself from his mount and threw his arms around his son.

"Jan, my boy!" he exclaimed. "Where have you been? We heard you were a prisoner in the Temple of Kali, and that you were to be sacrificed to the Black Goddess, so came as fast as we could in order to rescue you and Ramona. Have you seen her?"

"I have just escaped from the temple," Jan replied, "and know that Ramona is there, although I have not seen her. Is she in danger?"

"In danger!" exclaimed Trevor. "Jan, I'm surprised at you."

"I did not know but that she was there of her own free will," Jan answered.

"She was kidnaped by the maharaja, and he intends to either force her to marry him or kill her. Didn't you see the maharaja?"

"I have seen nothing of him," Jan replied. "The temple enclosure is large, and there are many buildings. He may be there, for there were many soldiers armed with rifles, and had it not been for the darkness and the fact that they are such poor shots, I would not be alive to tell of it.''

''Half of our mission is accomplished by your safety,'' said Trevor, ''but we must now hurry to the rescue of Ramona.''

''I will ride the elephant,'' said Jan, ''and show you the way.'' He paused for a moment to greet Don Francesco. Then he signaled to Malikshah, and the big bull instantly lifted him to a seat on his head.

Jan and Sharma led the procession, which consisted of Trevor, Don Francesco, Mr. Whitaker and the British Resident's twenty Sepoys—brave fighters whom Whitaker assured his companions were worth at least a hundred of the maharaja's guardsmen.

On reaching the bronze gate of the temple, Mr. Whitaker beat upon it with the butt of his pistol and demanded admission in the name of the British Government.

A shaven headed priest opened a small aperture in the gate and peered out at them. ''This is holy ground,'' he said, ''and no unbeliever can be admitted.''

''It seems you are ready enough to admit them when they are intended for sacrifice,'' said Whitaker. ''Open the gates and deliver to us the *memsahib* you hold prisoner here, or we will break them down.''

''There are no prisoners here,'' lied the priest, ''and it is against the law and contrary to the tenets of our religion for any *sahib* to enter this place.''

''Very well,'' said Whitaker,'' then we will enter without your leave.''

He backed his horse from the opening and motioned to Sharma.

"See what your elephant can do against those gates," she said. "Better pad her head first." Two of his men quickly brought saddle blankets, which were bound over Rangini's forehead.

At this moment a burst of rifle fire came from the loop holes above them and the two Sepoys fell to the ground. Their comrades instantly answered the fire, and screams of pain from inside the wall made it manifest that some of the shots had taken effect.

The Sepoys picked up their two fallen comrades and covered the retreat of Jan, Sharma and the three white men with their fire.

Whitaker ordered his warriors to deploy in a semicircle around the gateway and then took counsel as to what their next move should be. He had not expected armed resistance on the part of the maharaja, and knew that the potentate must be very desperate indeed to order his men to fire upon British soldiers.

While they were taking counsel as their next move, the keen eared Jan suddenly said, "I hear more horses coming—many of them."

"It must be that the maharaja has sent for help," said Whitaker. "We will have to withdraw or we will be surrounded and wiped out. Now I know why he so fearlessly ordered his men to fire upon us. It is his intention that not one of us shall live to tell the story."

CHAPTER XVIII

THE BABU'S LOOT

Despite the painful wound in his fat neck, Babu Chandra Kumar rode happily toward the railway station. Not one, but two money belts heavy with gold were buckled around his ample middle. And his greasy turban bulged with the wealth of rupees it could scarcely contain.

On arriving at the station he dismounted and handed the reins to Kupta.

"Gooptoo is very good donkey," he said. "How would you like to own him?"

"I would like very much to own him," Kupta replied.

"He is worth one hundred rupees, but since I like you so well I will sell him to you for fifty."

"Nay, I can spare but twenty-five for so small and mangy a beast," replied the hillman.

"Make it thirty-five," said the babu, "and he is yours."

Kupta removed his turban, fished out thirty-five rupees, and handed them to the babu. Then he untied the latter's battered suitcase and rusty old umbrella from the rear of the saddle and handed them to him.

"I hope we shall meet again soon, *babuji*," he said, and tears suddenly welled from his eyes. "We have been together a long time, now."

"I hope so, too, my brave comrade," the babu sniveled, tears rolling down his fat cheeks. But inwardly he was rejoicing, because he had only paid ten rupees for the decrepit donkey which the gullible Kupta had just purchased for thirty-five.

The little hillman mounted and rode away, turning several times to wave farewell.

Babu Chandra Kumar sighed, smiled, and picking up suitcase and umbrella, walked into the tiny railway station.

"When is next train for Howrah?" he asked the young babu in the ticket office, with a superior air.

"Next train will arrive in ten minutes," the clerk replied.

"Then sell me one second class ticket—"

He got no further, for at this moment he felt something sharp pricking him in the back. Turning, he beheld a huge scar-faced man with a flame-red hennaed beard—and his knees almost collapsed beneath him.

"*Adab babuji!*" rumbled Zafarulla Khan. "Will you come quietly, or shall I thrust the knife clear through you?"

"*Adab araz,*" replied the babu, turning pale and essaying a sickly smile. "Of course I will come with you. Am very glad to see you."

He waddled out of the station with the tall Pathan close at his side.

"Did you wish to speak to me privately?" he asked.

"*Very* privately," Zafarulla Khan told him. "This place will not do at all. It is entirely too public."

He took the babu's fat arm in his iron grasp and marched him down the road to the place where his men awaited him in a little secluded glade.

Zafarulla Khan prodded the money-laden midriff of the babu and chuckled.

"A fat sheep ready for the shearing," he said. Then he asked: "Will you remove those money belts yourself, or shall I take them off for you?"

"What money belts?" asked the babu, blandly.

"So! You are going to lie about it!" growled the Pathan, with a fierce look and a significant wave of the knife.

"No, I will take them off," said the babu hastily, unbuckling the two belts and dropping them at his feet.

"Pick them up, you swine," roared Zafarulla Khan.

The babu bent over to comply. As he did so, his turban fell off with a loud clink.

"Hah! What's this? By the beard of the prophet, on whom be peace and Allah's blessing! By the holy well of Zem Zem, and by the Hatim Wall! You have been hiding some money from me! I should cut off your head for this!"

The babu was trembling as if with the ague.

"Pray spare your humble and unworthy slave," he whined. "I was so frightened by that big knife of yours that I forgot about the few rupees in my turban."

One of the Pathans who had picked it up shook the last rupee from the babu's greasy headpiece. Then he clapped it back on his shaven head.

Zafarulla Khan buckled the two heavy money belts beneath his sash. The rest of the money was put into a saddle bag. All was to be divided later.

"Not only will we spare your life; we will see you off for Howrah," said Zafarulla Khan, grinning broadly. "We should be ungrateful swine, did we not see you off, after the magnificent and princely gift you have bestowed upon us in farewell."

The babu was hustled back to the roadway. The Pathans all mounted their horses, except Zafarulla Khan, who led his as he walked beside the babu.

Before they reached the station, the train pulled in, stopped for a moment, and rumbled on.

"You've missed your train," said Zafarulla Khan. "That's too bad. But the track is still there, and fortunately you still have your legs. If you will use them to good purpose, perhaps you may save your head."

The babu waddled into the station and recovered his suitcase and umbrella. Both were so shabby that no one had bothered to steal them.

The clerk looked at him curiously as he waddled out.

"Farewell, *babuji*," called Zafarulla Khan, as the babu started off down the track. "May good health and prosperity attend you."

Weeping copiously, the tears running down his fat jowls, the babu plodded doggedly away in the direction of Howrah, suitcase in one hand and umbrella in the other.

The Pathans laughed uproariously, as they watched him depart. Then Zafarulla Khan turned and swung into his saddle. He was about to give the command to ride away, when the words stuck in his throat. For a hundred Rajput warriors armed with rifles suddenly rode in upon them from all directions.

Their leader, a huge, black-bearded warrior, reined his mount to a halt beside that of the Pathan chieftain.

"*Salaam aleykum,* Zafarulla Khan," he said.

"*Aleykum salaam*, Mahmood," the Pathan replied. "Were you looking for someone?"

"*Ayewah!* We were looking, but our search has ended. You and your men will surrender your weapons and loot, and come with us at once."

Zafarulla Khan looked around at the menacing rifle barrels of the Rajputs, and knew that they meant business. He also knew that if he and his men resisted they would be shot down without mercy.

"In Allah's name," he asked, "What is the meaning of this? We are but peaceful horse traders who came down to the station to see a friend off."

"I saw you following your friend and guessed your purpose," said Mahmood. "You are under arrest for raiding the camp of the Maharaja of Varuda in British territory, and for abducting the *memsahib,* Ramona Suarez. Also, you have just committed a robbery in Rissapur territory. Now surrender at once, or it will be the worse for you."

Zafarulla Khan cringed and blustered by turns. He called upon all the Moslem saints and prophets to bear witness that he was innocent. But in the end he and his men were compelled to turn over their weapons and their loot.

Then, with their hands bound behind their backs, and their horses led by stalwart Rajputs, they rode back to Rissapur, the prisoners of its maharaja.

CHAPTER XIX

THE MIGHT OF KALI

Driven back from their position before the temple gate, and with a possible flank attack by the approaching horsemen imminent, Trevor, Don Francesco, Whitaker and Jan took council as to their next move.

Whitaker insisted that the maharaja would not have dared to order his men to fire upon British troops unless he was positive that none of the party would escape alive.

"Why, it would be suicidal for him," said the British resident. "He might be able to prove his innocence on the charge of kidnapping. For all we know, he may be the victim of a plot engineered by the priests of Kali. But he can never beat such a charge as this if one of us escapes alive. The conclusion is obvious."

"Whether the approaching horsemen are his men, or others," said Trevor, "we can do Ramona no good by waiting here. We must force our way into the temple somehow, and quickly, if we are to save her."

"I doubt that he would dare to go so far as to

sacrifice the girl to his hideous black goddess,'' said Whitaker. ''Why, if he should—''

He was interrupted by the booming of the huge gong within the temple.

''What's that?'' Trevor asked.

''It means that there is to be a sacrifice made to the Black Mother, *sahib*,'' a Sepoy replied.

''In that case we must get inside quickly,'' said Jan, ''for Ramona is in deadly danger.'' He turned to Whitaker. ''If you will keep the marksmen above the gate occupied, I'll try to crash through with Malikshah.''

''We can keep them occupied for a while,'' said Whitaker, doubtfully, ''but I don't know how long.''

''I'll ride with you, my boy, and shoot from the elephant's back,'' said Trevor.

''I, also,'' cried Don Francesco. ''It is my little daughter, my beloved baby, that these demons would torture and slay.''

Swiftly, with the help of Sharma, Jan bound a pad on the forehead of the huge bull. Then he mounted to Malikshah's neck. Another pad was strapped on the elephant's broad back, and on this Trevor and Don Francesco took their places, repeating rifles in their hands and pistols holstered at their hips.

At a word from Jan, the giant bull plunged forward.

''Commence firing,'' cried Whitaker.

Spurts of flame leaped out from the surrounding jungle as the eighteen remaining Sepoys went into action.

Malikshah charged up to the gate, the jungle man crouching on his neck and urging him forward, while Trevor and Don Francesco coolly picked off such turbaned heads as came within their line of vision. The elephant applied his head to the gate, and pushed. It was a strongly built gate, but could not resist the tremendous weight that the big bull hurled against it, and crashed inward at the first onslaught.

At this moment, the riders who had been heard at a distance some time before, and whom the British Resident had suspected of being the Maharaja of Varuda's men, came charging up, yelling and waving their wifles. They were Rajputs, and at their head rode Abdur Rahman, Maharaja of Rissapur.

As Malikshah went crashing through the gate into the temple enclosure, the Rajputs stormed in after him, deploying to the right and left, and shooting down guards and priests alike.

Jan guided the elephant straight across the gardens and up the steps of the temple. Straight through the great arched doorway he charged, and into the midst of a startled throng of priests, musicians and dancing girls.

Jan instantly caught sight of Ramona crouched against the bars of the cage, with the tigress springing toward her. Leaping to the platform, drawn sword in hand, he came up behind the girl just as the tigress reared up to seize her. He thrust his sword through the bars, straight at the black furry throat, and the black tigress, taken by surprise, sprang back with a snarl of pain and rage.

Jan did not bother to go to the gate—indeed, there was no time for that. Instead, he gripped his sword with his teeth, and seizing the two bars against which Ramona leaned half aswoon, he bent them apart, exerting the terrific strength which his splendid physique and jungle training had given him, caught the girl as she fell, and pulled her clear just as the tigress leaped for the second time.

The Maharaja of Varuda had risen and rushed toward the cage at this unexpected interruption of his bloody ceremony. As the tigress sprang out of the cage, he shouted:

"Slay them, O Black Mother! Rend their bodies and drink their blood! Show them the power and the might of Kali!"

The tigress, attracted by the sound of his voice, turned, then suddenly sprang straight for him, seized his face in her huge jaws, and bore him to the floor.

Harry Trevor whipped his rifle to his shoulder and fired two shots, one through her head and one through her heart. Without a sound she sank lifeless beside the body of her victim.

The Sepoys and Rajputs had meanwhile broken into the temple, striking down the priests and guards who attempted to halt them, and taking all others prisoners. The musicians and dancing girls were huddled into a corner like a flock of frightened sheep.

Trevor seized the dead tigress by the scruff of the neck, and dragged her away from the head of the maharaja. His face was gone—completely bitten away.

"God!" exclaimed Trevor. "God, what a sight!"

"It is judgment upon him," said Whitaker with a shudder. "He besought Kali to turn her might against us, and it was turned upon himself instead."

The maharaja seemed trying to speak. There

was a movement from the place that had once been his mouth, and a few bloody bubbles issued from the gaping wound. Then he shivered from head to foot and lay still.

"He's dead," said Don Francesco. "May God have mercy on his black soul."

Suddenly there was a cry of "Fire!" from one of the shrill voiced dancing girls, and a billowing cloud of smoke poured from the rear of the temple. In the battle which had just ended, some one had evidently knocked down a cresset behind the great black idol. Once started, the ancient, seasoned timbers burned like matchwood.

Still holding the senseless form of Ramona in his arms, Jan shouted a command to Malikshah. The huge beast lifted the two of them to his head, and led the swift exodus from the burning temple.

In the garden outside, the prisoners were herded together, and the warriors once more mounted their horses. Soon the temple became a roaring inferno of flame, which cast such a terrific amount of heat that it was impossible to remain within the temple enclosure.

In orderly array the Rajputs and Sepoys rode out with their prisoners. Pausing at some distance from the gate, they watched the progress of the fire for a time. It soon spread to the buildings constructed against the wall of the enclosure, and the leaping flames lit the night sky in the vicinity with a lurid radiance.

Abdur Rahman, Trevor, Don Francesco and Whitaker stood in a little group, watching the conflagration. Sharma, the better to see the fire, had retained his seat on the neck of Rangini.

Jan and Ramona sat together on the pad which

had been strapped to the broad back of Malikshah. Her head was resting on his shoulder and his face was very close to hers.

"Can you forgive me, Ramona," he asked, "for even thinking that night on the boat that it was you who tried to kill me?"

"Of course, beloved," she replied.

Their lips met, and the sly old Malikshah, who had lived among men for a hundred years, and had seen many generations of lovers, flicked an appreciative ear.

Trevor nudged Don Francesco.

"It seems that the love birds have made up their quarrel," he said.

"That is the way of all who truly love, amigo," replied Don Francesco. "We should congratulate them, but perhaps it will be best to do so later. One should not interrupt the course of true love at a moment like this."

THE END

GLOSSARY OF NAMES AND TERMS IN THE JAN NOVELS

Compiled by David Anthony Kraft

Key:

Otis Adelbert Kline wrote two books in this series, and they will be abbreviated as follows—JAN OF THE JUNGLE: **Jan**, and JAN IN INDIA: **JI**.

GEORGIA ADAMS—maiden name of Georgia Trevor; **Jan**.

ANGAD—a mahout in service of the Maharaja of Varuda; **JI**.

ANPU—deity or ancestor of Emperor Mena; **Jan**.

BATAU—a Satmuan patrolman; **Jan**.

CECIL BAYNE—British Resident of Rissapur; **JI**.

BLACK MOTHER—an appellation for Kali; **JI**.

BLACK ONE—a black tigress held in captive in the Temple of Kali, believed to be an incarnation of the goddess; **JI**.

BLACK TEMPLE, or PAGO-DA—the Temple of Kali in Varuda; **JI**.

BORNO—giant Haitian Negro sailor on *Santa Margarita* who became Jan's friend; **Jan**.

DR. BRACKEN — enemy of the Trevors; **Jan**.

BRAHM—Hindu god, the Creator; **JI**.

CHICMA—female chimpanzee, mate of Tichuk, like a mother to young Jan; **Jan**.

GANESHA—Hindu god of wisdom; **JI**.

GEORGIA A.—yacht owned by Harry Trevor; **JI**.

GOOPTOO—donkey originally belonging to Chandra Kumar; **JI**.

JAKE GRUBB—first mate of the *Santa Margarita*; **Jan**.

UNCLE HENRY — colored help at Dr. Bracken's Florida home; **Jan**.

HEPR—Great God of the Waters; **Jan**.

HERU—deity or ancestor of Emperor Mena; **Jan**.

HOUSE OF THE BLACK MOTHER—the Temple of Kali in Varuda; **JI**.

ISMAIL—a Pathan, companion of Mutiur Rahman and member of Zafarulla Khan's party; **JI**.

AUNT JENNY—colored help in Dr. Bracken's Florida home; **Jan**.

KAN—the mighty serpent, earthly representative of the god Quetzalcoatl; **Jan**.

KALI—the Great Goddess, wife of Siva; **JI**.

KOH KAN — yellow-skinned friend of Jan; Prince Koh of the House of Kan; **Jan**.

KEBSHU—a priest of Set, first assistant to Samsu; **Jan**.

GEMPA KETCHIL — Ma-layan for Little Earthquake: a.k.a. Jamila; **JI**.

ZAFARULLA KHAN—a giant, head of the Pathan cutthroats; **JI**.

CHANDRA KUMAR—a babu and treacherous servant of the Maharaja of Varuda; **JI**.

KUPTA—a hillman underling of Babu Chandra Kumar; **JI**.

LITTLE EARTHQUAKE— Gempa Ketchil; a.k.a. Jamila; **JI**.

PETE LITTLE — Seminole Indian killed by Dr. Bracken; **JI**.

PADRE LUIS—a missionary priest in the Amazon; **Jan**.

MAHADEVI—another appellation for Kali; **JI**.

MAHARAJA OF RISSAPUR —Abdur Rahman, arch-enemy of the Maharaja of Varuda; **JI**.

MAHARAJA OF VARUDA—treacherous Indian who also served as the secret High Priest of Kali; **JI**.

MAHMOOD—a Rajput warrior in service of the Maharaja of Rissapur; **JI**.

MALIK — old lion in Dr. Bracken's Flordia menagerie; **Jan**.

MALIKSHA — mighty bull elephant ridden by Jan; **JI**.

MARJANAH—an old English-speaking hag in service of the priests of the Temple of Kali; **JI**.

McGREW—captain of the *Georgia A.*; **JI**.

MENA—Emperor of Satmu; **Jan**.

ARTHUR MORRISON — Ramona Suarez's English tutor in South America; **Jan**.

MU-HAPI—twin mountain of Qer-Hapi in Satmu; **Jan**.

NEFERTRE—Empress of Satmu; **Jan**.

NELSON—second officer of the *Georgia A.*; **JI**.

PEBEK—a Satmuan patrolman; **Jan**.

PILATRE—High Priestess of Aset, Daughter of the Sun; Teta's daughter; **Jan**.

QER-HAPI—twin mountain of Mu-Hapi in Satmu; **Jan**.

QUETZALCOATL—serpent god of Central America; **Jan**.

ABDUR RAHMAN—Maharaja of Rissapur; **JI**.

MUTIUR RAHMAN—a Patman, member of Zafarulla Khan's party; **JI**.

RAJAM—a captain in service of Maharaja of Varuda; **JI**.

RANGINI—she-elephant ridden by Sharma; **JI**.

RE—Egyptian and Satmuan god of the sun; **Jan**.

RISSAPUR — maharajadom of Abdur Rahman; **JI**.

RUIZ—one of Don Francesco Suarez's boatmen; **Jan**.

SAMSU—High Priest of Set; **Jan**.

SANTA MARGARITA — a Venezuelan schooner; **Jan**.

FRANCESCO SANTOS — captain of the schooner *Santa Margarita*; **Jan**.

SARKAR—another mahout in the service of the Maharaja of Varuda; **JI**.

SATMU—city of the golden Sect of Re and lost colony of Mu; **Jan**.

SEBEK—great fish-reptile and earthly representative of the demon, Set; **Jan**.

SET—Egyptian and Satmuan god of evil; **Jan**.

SHARMA—young Indian boy and companion of Jan; **JI**.

SIVA—Hindu god, the Destroyer; **JI**.

SEÑORA SOLEDAD—Ramona Suarez's doting old duenna in South America; **Jan**.

FRANCESCO SUAREZ — *don* and foster-father of Ramona; **Jan, JI**.

ISABELLA SUAREZ—*doña* and foster-mother of Ramona; **Jan, JI**.

RAMONA SUAREZ — daughter of Mena and Nefer-tre; foster-daughter of Don Francesco and Doña Isabella, and bethrothed of Jan; **Jan, JI**.

Tehuti—a bird deity of Satmuans; **Jan**.

TEHUTI—a bird deity of Sat-muans; **Jan**.

TELAPU—son of Samsu, a coward; **Jan**.

TEMPLE OF KALI—hidden scene of foul rites in Varuda; **JI**.

TEMPLE OF SEBEK—home of the ichthyosaur to whom sacrifice often was offered; **Jan**.

TEMPLE OF SET—dedicated as place of worship to the black demon; **Jan**.

TEMUKAN—native city of Koh Kan; **Jan**.

TETA—High Priest of Asar; **Jan**.

THAKOOR—alleged High Priest of Kali; **JI**.

TICHUK—surly old male chimpanzee in Dr. Bracken's Florida menagerie, and mate of Chicma; **Jan**.

GEORGIA TREVOR—Jan's mother, formerly promised to Dr. Bracken; **Jan, JI**.

HARRY TREVOR — father of Jan, an American million-aire sportsman; **Jan, JI**.

JAN TREVOR—Jan of the

Jungle, named by Dr. Bracken for Jan ibn Jan, Arabic Sultan of the Evil Jinn; named Crown Warrior by Emperor Mena; son of Georgia and Harry Trevor, and bethrothed of Ramona Suarez; **Jan, JI**.

USEPHAIS — doctor in Satmu; **Jan**.

VARUDA—a maharajadom; **JI**.

VARUDAPUR — capital of Varuda; **JI**.

VISHNU—Hindu god, the Preserver; **JI**.

HENRY WESTGATE—English archeologist and explorer spending time in Satmu; **Jan**.

WHITAKER—British Resident of Varuda; **JI**.

ISHAAK EL YAHUDI— a Hebrew money-changer in Varudapur; **JI**.

YAMA—a rogue elephant; **JI**.

First Edition
1974

JAN IN INDIA by Otis Adelbert Kline with illustrations by Steve Leialoha and a foreword and glossary by David Anthony Kraft was published by Fictioneer Books, Ltd. Approximately 1500 copies of this first edition were produced by CSA Printing and Bindery, Lakemont, Georgia from 12-point Baskerville type on 60 lb. CSA Book Paper and bound in 10-point Carolina-coated cover stock.